PANIC
BUTTON

A gripping crime thriller full of twists

CHARLIE
GALLAGHER

Published 2017 by Joffe Books, London.

www.joffebooks.com

© Charlie Gallagher

ISBN-13: 978-1-912106-62-2

Dedicated to all those who put on a uniform and run towards what the rest of us are running away from.

No matter what, no matter when.

Author's Note

I am inspired by what I do and see in my day job as a front-line police detective, though my books are entirely fictional. I am aware that the police officers in my novels are not always shown positively. They are human and they make mistakes. This is sometimes the case in real life too, but the vast majority of officers are honest and do a good job in trying circumstances. From what I see on a daily basis, the men and women who wear the uniform are among the very finest, and I am proud to be part of one of the best police forces in the world.

Charlie Gallagher

Police Personal Radio (PR) System: Instruction of use Q&A.

Section 9.4: EMERGENCY BUTTON

Q. Where is the emergency button located on the Police radio unit?
A. The emergency button is located on the top of the handheld unit. It is coloured a bright red and is raised to allow easy and fast access when required.

Q. When should I press the red button?
A. In any situation when you require emergency assistance.

Q. What happens on the radio network when I press my red button?
A. When the emergency button is activated, that call takes priority on the network giving the user an open microphone for a ten-second period followed by a locally defined time for the control room to respond. All personal radio units set to the same channel will also vibrate and provide an audible alert to each user to the emergency button being pushed.

Q. What happens if I press my emergency button when the airwaves unit is switched off?
A. When the radio unit is switched off pressing the emergency button will still be effective. Please be aware that the emergency button function WILL NOT be effective if the battery is removed.

Q. Does the GPS system still assist with finding my location when the emergency button is pressed?
A. When the emergency button is pressed the Global Position System immediately increases in signal strength allowing the control room to accurately identify your position.

CHAPTER 1

It was 2:45 p.m. and the heat was still unbearable. It was nearly the end of the shift and Police Constable Matthew Riley was regretting his decision to step out of the air-conditioned interior of his police vehicle. He reached for the radio strapped to his chest, depressed the long button on its side and held it in front of his mouth. 'Charlie Bravo One, One, Control, can you TA me Canterbury Road please?' Riley received a tinny confirmation and twisted the button at the top to turn down the volume. The heat was thick, tangible almost, weighted down like an extra layer over the uniform that clung to the damp patch on his back. Riley pushed at the gate. It sprang shut with a sudden loud noise as he passed through and made his way up the steps to the door of number 17.

The place was unremarkable, set in a row of identical terraced houses. They were connected at the top, with interior space on the ground floor lost to narrow alleyways that gave access to the back gardens. These mostly harboured rubbish bins. Number 17 was presentable, the front garden was well kept and the thick hedge flourished, with recently trimmed and squared edges. Riley knocked twice on the blue wooden door. He pressed the doorbell and turned back towards the garden, where flowerbeds ran away from the house, full of colour. The dull roar of passing traffic sounded beyond the hedge.

Riley stood facing into the sun. His thick duty trousers, heavy stab vest and equipment belt absorbed the heat and spread the various damp patches. Sweat beaded on his forehead as he once again pushed the transmit button on his radio.

'Control — confirm the address the caller gave please.'

The reply was instant: *'Charlie Bravo One, One from Control, 17 Canterbury Road.'*

'Received that, Control. I've got no reply here. Go again with what was said on the call.'

'Bravo One, One, it's an abandoned three nines I'm afraid with very little information. We had a call asking for police, saying they were at 17 Canterbury Road, Langthorne and to come quick. The line was then cut. We've tried calling the number back but it's straight to answerphone and the number isn't linked to anyone on the system here.'

Riley exhaled. Another waste of his time. He stepped back from the house and peered up at the closed blinds in the top windows. At the side of the house was an alley that led through to the back with a gate at the far end blocking access and light. In contrast to the bright sunlight it was a dark tunnel. He tugged a bin out of the way and advanced a couple of feet into the gloom, where he stopped to allow his eyes time to adjust.

'Thank God you're here!' A voice. It was gravelly, as if the man had been waiting to speak for some time. Riley jumped a little. He heard movement. A man stepped out in front of him, he was just a shadowy shape.

'Was it you that called the police?' Riley asked.

'Yes. Keep your hands out to the side where I can see them.'

Riley was confused. 'Do what?'

'Keep your fucking hands *out*!'

Riley slowly lifted his arms out until he could feel the rough texture of the brick walls against his hands.

'Keep them there.' The tone was calmer now but still assertive.

'I came here to help, that's all.'

Riley was unfazed, confident of his ability to talk to people in all kinds of emotional distress. There was a six foot gap between them, the light wasn't sufficient to make out the man's features.

'Stay very still,' the man said. The gruffness in his voice indicated tension. The man was in his thirties, Riley guessed, certainly no younger, and had a local accent.

'I'm no threat, okay? You called me here. Tell me how I can help you.'

Without replying, the man began to lift something. Squinting, Riley could make out an extension lead. In an instant a bulb directly above Riley crackled into life, giving off a weak amber glow and revealing the man in front of him.

It also revealed the oversized pistol in his hand. He raised it, pointed it directly at Riley's forehead, where the sweat had now run into his eyes, making them sting. Riley put his hands out in front of him in a gesture of submission, his palms towards his aggressor, his body open.

'Keep your fucking hands against the wall!' The voice was stronger now. The man was wearing a black balaclava revealing just the smallest amount of white skin around eyes that looked at him steadily.

Riley returned his hands to the wall and tried to take his eyes away from the pistol. 'Look. I came here to see if someone needed help. I'm no threat to you, I just wanted to make sure everyone's okay.'

He noticed the man's mouth move behind the balaclava, as if he had licked his lips.

'You need to do exactly what I say if you want to stay alive. Do you understand?'

'Okay,' Riley said.

'When I tell you, and only when I do, I want you to press your emergency button on your radio, you understand?'

'Okay.' This suited Riley fine. He couldn't think of a time when he had wanted to press it more.

'When you press it, you have ten seconds to broadcast to your colleagues. You will read this out, word for word.' The man lifted a piece of white, A4 size paper with three lines written across it, in large letters. 'If you deviate from what is written on here I *will* shoot you in the face. Do you understand?'

Riley nodded. He focused on the paper and ran the words through his mind. He looked to where the sun leaked through gaps in the gate at the end of the alley. He longed to step back out into its warmth.

The man shifted his stance. 'Do it now!' He raised paper and pistol towards the officer. 'With your right hand, press the button then read the words slowly and clearly.'

Riley's movements were deliberate. He moved his hand to his radio, strapped to the left side of his chest. His eyes were wide and unblinking. His finger felt for the raised button on the top of the radio and he pressed it hard.

* * *

The police based at Langthorne covered an area of more than fifty square miles. A mix of motorways, towns, villages, and deep rural locations all had their own demands and problems. A team of eight response officers were responsible for its protection. The early turn, with the exception of Riley, had just gone off duty, and the late turn team were sitting in their briefing room at Langthorne Police Station. Pictures of the area's most wanted adorned the walls, along with their cautionary notices and types of criminality. Maps of the area were pinned to whiteboards, highlighting areas of concern or points where break-ins or assaults had taken place.

Sergeant Tim Betts sat at the front of the room. The police veteran with twenty-two years' service was trying to control the laughing hubbub of his team of eight, who were busy stuffing themselves with cake. Punishment for one of the group daring to have a birthday.

'Right!' Betts peered at the computer screen in front of him and selected the latest intelligence briefing. Projected onto a screen behind him, loomed a larger version of Langthorne's most wanted male, who had recently won a small victory in a chase with the traffic police. The picture was in close-up against a bright, white background. The face formed the main light source in the room, with the blinds shut against the heat and the lights turned off.

'Right. Listen in.' Betts fought down a laugh as he looked at one of his officers who was scraping fresh icing off his glasses.

Suddenly, each radio emitted a double beep and vibrated against their chests. Like everyone else in the room, Betts knew that emergency button activations were rare, mainly because they represented the point where a police officer had lost control, and immediate assistance was needed. Some of the officers got to their feet, picking up the car keys they had just been given by the departing early shift. Others sat up in their seats, dropping cake onto the table. They all had a tight feeling in their stomachs. Sergeant Betts bent over his radio and listened intently to the transmission. He twisted the volume button, unclipped his radio from its holder and lifted it to his ear. The occupants of the meeting room waited.

Next door, in the canteen, a tactical team had convened for a cup of tea. Having successfully completed a raid on a cannabis factory, they were putting off the inevitable paperwork that would follow. Now they focused their attention on their radios. The newest member of the team, who was responsible for the tea, had stopped the bubbling urn mid-flow. His cup was half full and he held it under the tap as they waited for the caller to begin.

Upstairs, the area commander was sitting in her office. Largely unused, her radio sat in its charging cradle. It shook and beeped, and the display glowed red. She dropped her pen, straightened her back and stared at it.

On a busy road, a firearms team passing through the area had stopped a young lad in a Citroën Saxo. He had been conversing on his mobile phone so intently that he had failed to see the marked patrol vehicle driving alongside him. He stood now on the hard shoulder, apologetic, shrugging his shoulders, but he was no longer the focus of attention. Both officers standing with him had bent their heads close to their radios, and one had jammed a finger in his ear in an attempt to block out the traffic noise. They waited.

* * *

At the force control centre, Sally Hennessy had been slumped in her chair — a position her chiropractor had told her to avoid. She lifted her headset and rubbed beneath the rubber pads over her ears. It had been a long shift and all three of her screens had been worked hard. The government cuts imposed on the police service meant that she was looking after a far larger area than ever before, including more police officers, each of whom was very much used to having their orders obeyed. She'd had just about enough of being bossed about and was looking longingly at a clock on the wall facing her. Another minute ticked away and then all three of her screens suddenly flashed bright red, and an audible alarm confirmed that someone had pressed for assistance. Off to her right she was aware that the control room inspector had turned towards her station. Sally's middle screen revealed the source of the call as PC Riley. The GPS system had already confirmed his exact location. Sally sat up straight, replaced her headset, and waited.

There was something unusual about this transmission. Normally, pressing the "panic button," as it was often referred to, would provide just that — a panicked update from an officer grappling with an offender, giving chase, or being chased. It would often be breathy, with the officer unsure where they were or in what direction they might be travelling, and it would be down to the control centre to pick up the pieces after the ten-second transmission and direct in all the available resources. This transmission, however, was clear and unhurried, as if the officer was standing still, pronouncing every word with deliberate care:

'A man is standing in front of me with a gun. He has a message for us all. He says that he will come for us. He will come for all of us one by one. Until it is finished.'

There was a pause. The screens on all the radios returned to black, their lights extinguished. The ten seconds had elapsed and officers across three towns tried to put a meaning to the words. Still nobody moved.

* * *

'Press it again.' The man dropped the paper and his hand moved to support the one holding up the weapon.

'And say what?' Riley stammered. Now he was afraid. The meaning of the words he had just read out had begun to sink in.

'Press the fucking button!' His tone had hardened. The man took a step towards him but Riley did not move away, he was frozen to the spot. His finger found the red button and he pushed it again.

* * *

All over Langthorne and in the surrounding areas radios shook, then hissed as the microphone stayed open. At force control centre, three screens flashed red. The voice this time was very different, it carried fear and uncertainty. It was quieter, the words directed away from the microphone. 'What do you want me to say now? I've done what you said!'

At the sound of the gunshot, Tim Betts jumped in his seat. Sally Hennessy emitted a yelp and knocked over her pen pot. The area commander stared wide-eyed at her radio. On the A20 dual carriageway, two officers looked at each other. In the canteen, half a cup of boiling water fell and shattered on the floor. When the second shot sounded, Betts closed his eyes, and lowered his head. For a few moments, Langthorne's entire police force froze.

CHAPTER 2

Inspector Nigel Harman was the first at the force control centre to move. The voices calling over the air, increasingly agitated, were initially met with silence.

'Sally!' Harman called out and she turned glassy eyes to the inspector. He could see she was really struggling. Her mouth lolled slightly open and she offered a desperate shake of her head.

'I'm sorry,' she said.

'Sally, let me take the air for a sec, just to give you a break.' She stood up, headphones ready in her outstretched hands. The inspector took hold of them as the voice of Tim Betts came back through, the tension clear in his tone.

'*Control, this is Charlie Bravo Two Zero, can you please hold off on sending officers to PC Riley's location, and can you resource any firearms officers? We don't know what we have.*' The radio fell silent for just a second before the same voice was back with instructions. '*And Control,*' Betts said, sounding a little breathless, '*Can we keep trying to raise him, please?*'

Harman took a seat, and sliding the headphones over his ears, pushed at the foot pedal that allowed control room operatives to cut over anyone else. It gave him the air.

'This is Inspector Harman at FCC. All officers are to remain clear of Canterbury Road, that is *all* officers are to remain clear of Canterbury Road.' The inspector paused with his foot planted on the pedal so no one else could cut in. Everyone would have heard him exhale a long breath before he spoke again. 'PC Riley, PC Riley, this is Inspector Harman for a welfare check.' He released the pedal, his eyes closed and he put his hands together in silent prayer.

There was no response.

'PC Riley!' the inspector shouted, 'Matthew. If you can hear me, please let me know any way you can.' He allowed another pause, longer, his head heavy on his shoulders. He spoke again, his voice quieter now, but still determined. 'Don't worry, lad. We're coming to get you.'

He released the pedal and sat up straight. He shouted at a woman working a nearby desk. She had risen to her feet and, like most people in the office, was staring over at the inspector. 'Rachel! I need ambient listening on Riley.'

The woman nodded and turned back to her desk. She was clumsy as she typed. After a few more seconds she held out a set of headphones for her boss.

'Put it on speaker,' he ordered, wanting to stay where he was in case his officer responded. Ambient listening was an option that needed the authorisation of an inspector. It was a way for the control centre to open the microphone of any individual officer's radio and listen to what was happening. It was mainly used in hostage situations, but it could also be effective for finding out what was going on when an officer wasn't responding to their radio. It was so rarely used that the inspector had almost forgotten about it.

In a hiss of white noise the speakers came to life. Harman peered around at the silent faces. The office normally buzzed. Like any busy call centre environment, it was noisy and intense, with up to forty people talking at any one time into microphones and telephones. Now they all stood still, waiting, with just the low buzz of call alerts backing up.

A breath sounded from the speakers. It was shallow, quick and short, but Harman bit his lip and hope seeped into the room. The second breath was quick to follow, and with it a distinctive noise, a rattle. Harman had heard it twice before during his time in the forces, from men suffering gunshot wounds to the chest. Both times the men were breathing their last.

* * *

Police Community Support Officer Jan Thomas had never been any good at monitoring her radio. Over the din of the primary school spilling out its chattering, laughing kids, she heard the distant sound of sirens, and her hand went to where her radio *should* have been. Sirens were hardly unusual but this was maybe the fifth or sixth one in the last fifteen minutes and Jan was beginning to think that something big might be going on. She cursed under her breath as she realised that for the umpteenth time she must have left the radio in her vehicle. She walked back to her car just as the latest siren, a high-revving police emergency response vehicle, flashed past. Its lights and sounds seemed somehow more intense than usual. Certainly the driver was not slowing up for the school and the elderly lollipop man in his oversized high-visibility jacket offered a scowl and a shrug. Her radio was on. She scooped it up and spun the dial on top to increase the volume. She found silence and checked the display to ensure she was on the right channel. She could hear more sirens in the distance, up on the bypass over the top end of the town.

'What's going on?' A thirty-something woman with fashionable short hair and a pretty face spoilt by heavy makeup stood nearby. Her six-year-old daughter squirmed in her grip.

'I haven't heard anything major,' replied Jan, which was not a lie and far better than admitting she hadn't a clue.

'So why so many police cars?' the woman persisted.

'I really don't know. I'm trying to listen.' Jan motioned at her radio and turned her considerable bulk aside. She was always irritable when she was too hot and she was even more flustered at being caught out by not exactly having her finger on the pulse. The woman took the hint and dragged her child away towards their car. In an attempt to avoid more questions, Jan walked over to where a separate building that housed the gym stood on the edge of the playground. She lifted her radio to her ear and was listening intently when the double doors to the gym were suddenly flung open.

'Excuse me. Are you a police officer?'

Jan recovered from her fright. 'Oh, well no. I'm the community support officer. Can I help?'

The man filling the doorway had bright, intense eyes. He was maybe ten years younger than Jan, and good-looking.

His smile widened. 'Ah, so you're still part of the same team. I'm sure you can help. I do maintenance here. I'm due to work in the gym but there's an unattended bag. I'm sure it's just one of the kids leaving their packed lunch, but I wondered if you have any procedures for this type of thing. I mean, you never know these days!' He turned sideways, holding the door. Jan thought he might have winked.

'Well, I'd best have a quick look.' Jan smiled back and stepped past him into the hall. Her eyes moved around the sparse interior. The newly built extension still smelt of wood and polish, its bars and ropes hugged the walls and hung from the ceiling. Various types of ball littered the ground. The black holdall looked out of place and Jan took a step towards it, walking through whirling dust lit up by strips of sunlight. The doors behind her clicked shut. The only sounds were her echoing footsteps, and those of the man following her.

Jan suddenly felt uncomfortable. The hall fell silent and she turned around. The smiling man now fixed her with a cold stare. He held the oversized barrel of a handgun inches from her forehead.

'Move or say anything and I will shoot you in the face. Do you understand?'

Jan was incapable of doing either of those things. Her legs felt like lead and her mouth hung slightly open.

'Listen to me.'

'Don't hurt me,' managed Jan. She shut her eyes tight, exposing the laughter lines across her plump cheeks.

'You need to listen *very carefully* to me. Do as I say and you won't be hurt, do you understand?'

Jan kept her eyes closed and her head jerked in a nod.

'Open your eyes and look at me.'

After a second or two Jan did as she was told. The man had stepped back, the weapon slightly lowered. He held up an A4 piece of paper with three lines of typed text in a large font. 'I want you to press your red button. Then read these words slowly and clearly into your radio. Can you do that?'

In a mumble, Jan read them out, stumbling over the words. She had no idea of their meaning.

'You need to do it *slower*. Slower and clearer so it makes sense, so they can send help. Can you do that?' The tone had changed again, it was almost supportive, encouraging.

Jan nodded. 'I can . . . I can. Please don't hurt me.'

'Do this for me and you won't get hurt. Now, press the button and read the words.'

Jan shut her eyes again and felt for the button on her handset. It was a small round button, set next to the aerial.

Her finger rested on it, her eyes opened wide and she pressed.

* * *

Canterbury Road, Langthorne. It tore directly through the heart of the town, a major artery for cars and foot traffic travelling in both directions. The 200 metre cordon either side of the house where PC Riley had last transmitted from was causing havoc. The scene was a confused mixture of annoyance, distress and hurried instructions, all played out in front of a live audience in thirty degree heat.

It was approaching half past three, and there was not a cloud in the sky to offer protection from the unrelenting sun. Men in uniform had their tongues hanging out like dogs as they manned the cordon. Their hi-vis tabards dazzled like the sun itself. Others stood behind their shields, gripped their weapons, and prepared to take control of number 17. Armed police were approaching the target address from all angles. They were all in black, clutching assault rifles and with full ballistic vests and helmets. A helicopter accompanying their approach thumped out a bass-line. It had been over the house within seven minutes of the shooting. No one had seen anyone leave the house, no one knew where Riley had fallen.

The tactical commander on the ground was Sergeant Hughes. He communicated by signals with the team he led on the black side (back) of the property, who readied themselves for an armed entry. The team on the white side (front) would wait for the sound of six-bang grenades before entering. Five riflemen with long-range sniper rifles covered the teams from every angle. They stood propped up at windows in the homes of willing neighbours thrilled to be involved in the drama.

Sergeant Hughes had received information from other neighbours that the occupants of 17 Canterbury Road were Jack and Jenny Hughes: a middle-aged couple who, three months earlier, had made their final mortgage repayment and were on a Mediterranean cruise to celebrate. They would be returning home via the port of Dover in five days' time. The current occupant, and the threat they presented, was completely unknown.

Hughes' raised fist was the signal for the team to freeze in silence. A three-tone on the radio had confirmed that the white side team were in position. Hughes and his team on the black side were also ready, if a little vulnerable in the long, well-kept garden bereft of any real cover. He lowered his fist and the team moved in. Hughes was in the lead, his rifle against his shoulder, gazing down the barrel. His team followed suit. A short distance from the door they broke into a run. Hughes stopped suddenly and dropped to his knees, his weapon pointing at the double patio doors that were their target. A figure ran past him to his right, holding a solid steel battering ram known as the "enforcer." He swung it backwards as he neared the door, and then brought it forward with perfect timing, connecting with the equivalent of three tons of focused force on an area the size of an orange. The frame offered little resistance and swung inwards hard, hitting the interior wall. An expensive-looking wooden slatted blind was shaken free, to be trampled to bits by the boots of six armed men.

Hughes was first in. He pulled the pin on his six-bang and threw it to the far side of the house. Amid the sounds of breaking glass the men shouted 'Police!' The six-bang ran its fuse and detonated, leaving nothing but scorch marks on the carpet. The team on the white side smashed in through the front door as the black team began to ascend the stairs. Still no contact with any hostiles. Hughes took a split second to assess the stairs through a sweat-splattered visor. He threw a second six-bang, which looped over the banister and collided with the wall before bouncing to rest on the thick carpet. By the time he had reached the top, the distraction grenade was already firing. It was a textbook operation.

The levels of noise and confusion as they swept through the house would most likely have caused any armed man on the property to cower under a bed. But there was no armed man, nor was there a fallen officer.

They returned to the living room, where Hughes gave a succinct and disappointed update on the radio. He pulled off his helmet and flash hood, and exhaled in relief. His team all followed suit and were all struggling to think of something to say when, suddenly, all their radios emitted a double beep.

For the second time that day an officer had pushed their panic button.

* * *

'None of you are safe or will be spared.' Jan's voice came out weakly. Terrified. 'One by one, I will take your lives.' She gripped the radio tightly, her knuckles white. She paused and whimpered as her brain made sense of the words. She looked past the paper at the man behind it. The bastard's lips had contorted into a smirk. He was enjoying this. 'Oh God,' murmured Jan. A tear ran down her cheek and found her lips. Her radio returned to black. Her ten seconds were up. The man appeared to know it and his eyes flicked from her to the screen, and back. Jan was unable to look away.

'Press it again. Say the words on the paper. Or die.'

She looked at the paper. Her hand was almost frozen around the radio and it took real effort to move her finger over the button. She pressed down on it.

In Langthorne, everyone stood still. Again, they all waited.

Jan read the last four words through her tears: "Like you took mine."

There was no pause for effect. The airwaves reverberated with two gunshots, followed by a thud and scraping noise. Jan's final transmission was over.

CHAPTER 3

In the nearest town to Langthorne, Sergeant Freddie Lee stood beside his marked motorcycle resting on its stand. The tank pinged and groaned. The long shift was nearly done. The sergeant sucked at a fast-melting ice cream which had run onto his knuckles. He crunched the last of the cone as constable Jack Leslie pulled up on his own cruiser. Freddie smiled at his colleague, who rested his own bike over to one side and pulled his helmet off. His hair was slicked flat against his skull.

'Fancy you arriving second.'

Jack made a point of gazing beyond the ice cream van at the beach, where the English Channel lapped at glittering pebbles in a haze of heat.

'It's a beautiful day for a slow ride, Sergeant. I don't race until I have to.'

'No one said you had to, Jack. If you're tired of losing just let me know.'

'You really are the smuggest man alive! Shall we just get this done then? Much as I love standing in the baking heat wearing all leather and talking shit with you, Sergeant, I've got a cold beer in my fridge that's calling to me.'

Freddie pulled his gloves back on over sticky hands. 'Right fork aren't I today? Not that it matters.'

Jack patted down his helmet and lifted the visor to reply. 'Yeah. You be careful on those bends.'

Both bikes fired and throbbed. The sergeant led the way away from the coast and through a couple of sets of traffic lights until they were able to ride side by side going up the hill that led out of Hythe. This was the starting point of their standard race to a lorry park around three miles distant. Freddie was two to one up in a four-day shift pattern, and was feeling confident of cementing his victory.

The starting point was just after the speed camera on London Road, where the road split into two evenly distanced routes. The winner would be the rider who negotiated their route the quickest before they could merge again. The speed camera edged past, the white distance markers on the road bumped slightly under Freddie's tyres and he leaned to take the right fork as his colleague accelerated straight on up the long hill.

The surface of the road was clear and the grip was good. Freddie made it to the first tight left, his left knee pointed downwards for balance, before a twist of the accelerator brought him back up straight. He opened up a little in second gear and moved into the correct position on the road for a long sweeping left. He brought the BMW over to the middle of the road so the white lines vibrated through his tyres and got his braking done early. He felt the weight of the bike move forward, and he let go of the brake and pulled down left. He grinned, feeling thin branches bounce off his shoulder, hearing them ping off his helmet. He hugged the left bank and the road in front revealed itself as he swung round into a longer straight. Then he saw a flash of sunlight off metal twenty metres in front of him on the opposite side of the road. A figure limped towards him down the middle of the road, one arm raised. Freddie stood hard on the rear brake, and the bike skidded to a stop.

The scenery that had been a blur of green became woodland, where broad trees shook their leaves gently in the warm breeze. Freddie could now make out a racing bike lying on its side on the grey tarmac. The bike was painted black with a bolt of lurid green on the tank. Freddie was not a fan of this type of bike and often mocked Jack for owning a similar one. At least the rider was in full leathers, they were cracked black and he still wore a matching, dark helmet.

Freddie sized him up. He was of a medium build, and limped as though he might have had a painful fall. Freddie pulled off his helmet to ask if he could be of assistance. This road was popular with bikers, and accidents on bends that had been misjudged or underestimated were common. At least the man didn't appear to be seriously injured.

Freddie flicked a switch on his handlebar that activated red and blue lights pointing to the rear. The bike hummed gently as it idled. 'Hello, what happened?'

The man limping towards him had his visor down.

Freddie leaned over the bike towards him to try and prompt a response. 'Are you ok?' The man still said nothing. Freddie noticed that his limp seemed to be improving, if not disappearing, as he watched. He tried again. 'Did you hurt your leg?'

The man stopped a couple of metres short of him. One arm came up from behind his back, and Freddie found himself staring at a large handgun. He struggled to find words that were relevant to this situation. His hands went out towards the gunman. The movement was instinctive, desperate.

Two bullets, one a split second after the other, smashed through the outstretched palms and penetrated the high-visibility vest and hardened leather chest plate like they weren't there. The bullets exited through Freddie's upper back, where one stopped deep in a tree and the other spun off into the woods behind. Freddie had been standing astride his bike, and now the BMW fell, taking him with it.

He felt no pain, nor could he move any part of his body. His breathing was becoming harsher, and every breath felt like it was crushing his heart. The man stood over Freddie and then dropped to one knee, placing the pistol on the ground. Freddie was aware of a hand fidgeting around his collar where his microphone was clipped. Then he saw a gloved finger find the red emergency button that was prominent on his handlebars and connected to the police radio. He pushed it firmly.

Less than two miles away and at nearly 100 mph, Jack Leslie's helmet emitted two loud beeps and he felt a vibration against his right ear and cheek. He eased up on the throttle and the bike slowed. Jack dipped his head as he tried to make out the transmission but all he, and the rest of the traffic team could hear, were the last breaths of their friend and colleague.

CHAPTER 4

'So what do you know, Ian?'

Detective Sergeant Ian Cutter had made a promise to his wife and family that he would give up smoking, but it was not going well. He had finally agreed a cut-off date, which had fallen two days before being put in charge of a major incident that was still unfolding. His mood when he came in to work his late shift had not been good. It was to become considerably blacker.

'What do I know?' Cutter repeated back at Detective Inspector Ross Price, his boss and the man responsible for landing him with the investigation. 'What do I know?' he said again, his voice rising. 'We have a nutter with a gun, who hates the police and anyone associated with them. We have three officers dead, three scenes manned by armed officers and we have a state of emergency. Does that sound about right?'

The inspector shook his head and puffed out his cheeks. 'You seem to have the crux of it. I've just come from a meeting where a call was made to ground all operational officers. That is uniform or otherwise, so we have an investigation that we can't actually start investigating yet. We're losing witnesses and opportunities with every passing minute.'

'So much for the golden hour principle.'

'I've never seen anything like this, Ian. This meeting, it was senior officers, they're scared right now and no one knows the next step.'

DS Cutter was still standing in Price's office. He hadn't felt like sitting. On his walk through the station he'd noted that none of the police officers who now flooded the station were seated either. They seemed to be walking the corridors in a daze, still wearing their full kit. Cutter knew that coppers developed strong bonds quickly, heightened by a "them and us" attitude. He'd seen this throughout his thirty years of service. The three victims were well known and well liked. The station was a very strange and very tense place to be and everyone was waiting for some sort of direction from the office where Cutter was now standing.

Both men were silent, not knowing what to say next. Cutter and DCI Price had worked together for two years, and although Cutter was fifteen years older, he had come to like and respect his boss.

'Right, let's go back over exactly what we have.' Price leaned on the back of his chair and motioned for Cutter to sit down. 'And we'll take them one at a time.'

Cutter reached for an A4 notebook that had been new this morning and was almost half full already. 'First victim was a response officer, PC Matthew Riley. We know that he was sent to an abandoned 999 call at the top of Canterbury Road. We now know that the property is empty and the owners are abroad. We've run them through the box and they've got no police record between them at all. The husband was a victim of a crime once, that's it.'

'A victim of what?' Price said.

'Criminal Damage. Some kids ran over his car in the early hours in 2006 — minimal damage, no offender, it was written off.'

'Associates?'

'Nothing on our systems. There's no intelligence about them at all. From what we can tell from the neighbours they're a decent couple, both retired, who now travel regularly. We have located a son who lives in the town and we're planning on speaking to him today. Beyond that we will be waiting for the couple to return.'

'There's nothing there, is there?' Price seemed to be thinking out loud.

'No. The shooting happened in an alley that runs down the side of the house. I'm pretty sure that the offender chose it because it suited his needs. It was secluded, but still central and nothing at all to do with the occupants of the address.'

'*His* needs?'

Cutter nodded. 'We can be pretty sure of that. Statistically it's most likely, also the voice from the very first call is masculine.'

'We have a voice?'

'A distorted one. Only subtly, and not enough to raise the call-taker's suspicion, but enough to make it difficult to identify or match up. We're still working on that though.'

The DCI exhaled loudly and rubbed at his mouth. 'You said he was looking for somewhere central? You think the location is relevant?'

'This guy's shot and killed three police officers in broad daylight. The locations were chosen in order to make the maximum impact. The first two especially — both were outside, both in busy areas and the choice of a school really gets the locals worried. The third one could have been an opportunist attack, the MO differed a little.'

'Differed how?' asked Price.

'Sergeant Lee was shot and then his button was pushed, probably by the offender, to allow us to hear him die.' Price's jaw tensed and Cutter continued. 'The previous two victims had been forced to read out a prepared script. The shooter left both pieces of paper lying with the victims. It is possible that he hadn't planned the third and just took his opportunity.'

Price stood up. He paced over to a map of Langthorne and surrounding areas, with coloured lines and shading marking out different territories. 'Where are the locations in relation to each other? Are we sure the timings make sense and have we any theories about how he's travelling?'

Cutter followed his boss over to the map and pointed at Canterbury Road, which was on the north side of the town. 'Riley was here just before three this afternoon.' Cutter's hand moved further up the map, over a large roundabout at the very top of the town, and continued up to the village of Hawkinge. This place had undergone recent and massive expansion via new-build housing and was now almost a town. It was perhaps a five-minute drive from Canterbury Road in heavy traffic. St Winifred's School was on the southwest side of the village and was almost brand new, the map showed nothing more than a large green field. 'Jan was here. The school kicked out at three fifteen and she pressed her button at three twenty-three.' Cutter's hand swept across the map, resting at the north side of Hythe. This was a seaside town that lay west of Langthorne and was linked to it by a stretch of exclusive properties, bars and restaurants that either directly fronted the sea or were secreted in the steep, hilly landscape, affording their owners privacy and an enviable view across the channel. Cutter was pointing at the rural area, twenty minutes from the centre of Langthorne, where the houses were mainly farms or guesthouses and the scenery was woods and rolling fields. 'And here, just after four, was where Sergeant Lee was attacked,' he continued.

'So it's all possible within the timeline.' Price turned away from the map and looked out of his window, down onto a yard full of immobile police vehicles.

'It works, yes. The first and second attacks are tight at that time of day. You could do the journey but it must have taken time to do some preparation, to pick his spot. Certainly it wouldn't be a problem if there were multiple offenders.'

Price spun round to face Cutter. 'You think that's possible?'

Cutter nodded. 'We can't rule anything out. This would have taken some planning and the logistics are much easier if you're talking about a group.'

Price turned back to the window, his words directed out to the silent yard. 'A group. You think we should be considering a terrorist group?'

'We just don't know,' Cutter said. It was not a day for comforting platitudes.

'You need to get in with your team. How many have you got?'

'I have seven detectives and as many uniform officers as I could ever need. There are people coming in on their days off to help out. Everyone wants this bastard caught, and right now we're just sitting them down in rooms around Langthorne House.'

'Best place for them right now. Until we can get a hold of this threat I can't have anyone out, uniform or not'

'You're right,' Cutter agreed. Sensing that the meeting had come to a natural conclusion he said, 'I'll keep you informed, sir. We've set up in the canteen, fifth floor, it's the only room with enough space. We've set an area aside for you with a terminal and a few bits so you can be in among it. There'll be a lot of work being done — and there's the bonus of the coffee machine.'

Price was still peering out of the window but turned on his heels as Cutter made to leave, unsure if his boss had heard him.

'Ian,' he said, and the sergeant stopped. 'I need to be calling the chief constable, the chief superintendent and all sorts of spaghetti right away and I need to be pretty straight about the situation we find ourselves in. So that I haven't misunderstood — this isn't over, is it? I mean, based on what we know.'

Cutter bit his bottom lip. 'At this stage, we have to assume that it's just beginning.'

* * *

Cutter waited for the door to close behind him before exhaling loudly. The sun had fallen low in the sky. He checked his watch — 8.20 p.m. His shift was due to finish at ten but he had already phoned his wife to tell her he would be home much later. She was accustomed to such calls and didn't even ask why. The life of a major crime sergeant rarely fitted into a neat shift pattern.

Cutter stepped into the clunking lift and his finger hovered over the number 5. While he hesitated, a woman entered, smiled at Clutter and began to peel yellow rubber gloves from her hands.

'Where to, love?' Cutter said.

'Ground, please. Time for cigarette.' Cutter thought her accent might be Polish. She gave another smile.

Cutter narrowed his eyes. 'You don't have a spare, do you? Only I've given up.'

'You give up?' she said.

'If my wife asks I have.'

The woman took a second, then grinned at him. 'Naughty man!' Long blonde hair fell over her attractive face as she reached into her pocket for her cigarette packet. She tugged the box open and held it out to Cutter.

Cutter pressed the button for the ground floor. 'Thank you. Today I really need one.'

'You have bad day?'

'You could say that, yeah. The whole force has had a shocker.'

'I hear bad things. People hurt.'

'Badly hurt.'

'Why?' Jana looked genuinely upset.

'That question is the reason I need this cigarette. They've put me in charge of finding out.'

She dropped her gloves into a bucket at her feet, lifted her hands to her hair and began to tie it up. Her bust strained against her polo shirt, which had "Jana" stitched on one side of her chest and "Prestige Cleaning Services" on the other. Cutter kept his eyes focused on the mirrored wall. On the ground floor, Jana lifted her bucket out of the lift and set it down. 'I come back, you need lighter too?'

Cutter tapped the pocket where he usually kept his much-loved Zippo, and of course his wife had removed it. 'I guess I do.'

'You follow me.' Jana walked towards the side exit of the building and Cutter followed, now able to admire her from behind much less surreptitiously.

CHAPTER 5

It was close to 3 a.m. and Langthorne seemed to be covered by a muggy blanket as it slept. Finally Cutter was able to step out of the station and leave for home. It had been hard to resist the temptation to simply kick off his shoes and lie down on the couch in the canteen.

Cutter stopped at his car and watched brake lights flicker in the distance. The last of his team of detectives was slipping away for the few hours' sleep they would get before returning to pick up where they had left off.

And where had they left off? Cutter sighed and expelled smoke from another scrounged cigarette. He went back over what they had done since the shootings occurred. Not much. In his career, he'd run nine murder investigations and basically they all followed the same pattern: the killer would do the deed, then try to get as far away from the victim and the scene of the crime as possible. It was then the turn of the police to conduct a slow, methodical and painstaking investigation, whereby the offender could be identified with evidence that would be compelling enough for a conviction in a court of law. He'd had his successes, probably more than most, but this case was very different. This killer was not covering his tracks or running away from the murder scenes. Instead, he seemed intent on creating more.

The night was still. Cutter leaned on the nearly new BMW 5 Series that he'd bought recently when his pension had paid him his lump sum. He had his hands in his pockets, the cigarette still between his lips. When he'd purchased the car, he had sworn to anyone who would listen that he'd "had enough." Now that he had served his time, he would not be returning to Lennokshire Police. The thought of actual retirement, however, had caused him to panic. His return to his vacated role as Major Crime Detective Sergeant had been so speedy that he had been able to smile knowingly at the cleaner who walked past him, carrying the wrapper from his "Happy Retirement" cake the day after his party on the top floor of Langhorne House. Perhaps it was the cake that prompted him, but Cutter had taken a moment to look in the large, stained mirror of the toilet in the police station bar. He'd run the words back through his mind, allowing himself for the first time to explore their meaning. "Happy retirement," he'd said out loud to his reflection, "what does it mean?" Cutter had known the answer all along, and, waving away another celebratory whiskey, had marched straight to DCI Price. The conversation had lasted sixty seconds. Price knew better than to ask Cutter if he was sure, and instead nodded his approval, broke into a smile and offered his hand.

That conversation had taken place just seven weeks ago. Cutter had never looked back, never wished that he had stepped away from it all and taken his retirement, never lost the confidence that he could deal with whatever might come through the door. Until now.

Cutter discarded the cigarette, found a packet of mints and slid into the driver's seat of the BMW. It rumbled into life with the push of a button. It was the 3.0 litre petrol model, a car he had admired from a distance for most of his adult life, and it had not disappointed. The menu screen in the centre console beamed a welcome, and the chair that had moved back to allow the driver a more comfortable entry now eased forward to Cutter's pre-programmed position. The headlights switched themselves on without the nuisance of having to press a button, illuminating the car park.

Cutter didn't see the figure standing still and silent, directly in the path of the headlights. He selected drive and the car moved forward. Then his tired eyes picked out the shape of a man. Cutter's face flickered in confusion and his right foot found the brake. The car immediately expressed its concern for the environment by moving the gear to neutral and killing the engine, and the 3 a.m. silence returned to Langthorne. The figure didn't move. He was tall and slim, in dark clothing, his head covered by a hood. His hands were behind his back.

Cutter swore and reached down to switch his lights to full beam. He fumbled for a few seconds, and then looked up as the lights illuminated the figure in front of him. Cutter saw that the figure was wearing a full-face balaclava. He was awfully close now, close enough for Cutter to see the eyes squinting against the bright headlights. Cutter watched, immobile, as the man brought his hand from behind him and raised a pistol that gleamed in the headlights.

* * **

The man fired four silenced rounds in quick succession. Cutter had no time to form words, no time to try and save himself. The windscreen offered little resistance and three of the bullets found Cutter's chest, with the fourth embedding itself in the leather of the driver's seat. The man tugged the door open and held the weapon at head height, but there was no need. His victim lay still. His right arm had fallen from the steering wheel and hung out of the car.

The man tucked his weapon into his waistband. He pulled a police issue radio from a small, black rucksack that he carried. Somewhere in the town a bored and heavily armed night-duty constable started a transmission about sheep being loose on a main road. An emergency button activation cut him off.

After the ten seconds of silence was complete, the control centre staff looked at each other in confusion. How was it that the urgent assistance call had been totally silent, and had originated from Langthorne House police station itself? It would be a further four minutes before the source of the activation was discovered — time enough for the figure responsible to disappear among the darkened side streets that surrounded the station.

CHAPTER 6

DCI Price swept through the fifth floor of Langthorne House. His ashen face was mirrored by those of just about everyone he came into contact with. They silently stepped out of his way as he headed towards the incident room, recently set up in a canteen. A chair had been set aside for him, and a steaming cup of coffee stood on a dining table used for meetings. A number of people were sitting around it.

'Ross, welcome. Sorry about the wake-up call.' Price looked at the slim, immaculately dressed woman who was standing at the head of the table and who had used his first name.

'Ma'am,' he replied, but Chief Superintendent Helen Webb had already turned away to retrieve a notebook. She placed it on the table in front of her and lowered herself onto her seat, sighing and keeping her eyes down. She appeared to be struggling for a place to start.

'You all had a very similar phone call,' she managed. The five members of the senior management team who had arrived for the 6.30 a.m. meet, all nodded, Price included. 'You will know that we have suffered a fourth loss overnight, just a couple of hours ago in fact. Detective Sergeant Ian Cutter, shot and killed in front of this very building.' The people gathered around the table all knew of this but Helen's words still got a reaction. They shook their heads, there was a sharp intake of breath and even a gasp. Price looked at their faces. They were tense and angry, but there was something else there too: fear.

'The killing has enough similarities to the three shootings that occurred yesterday to suggest that Ian's death was the fourth at the hands of the same individual,' Helen continued. 'Ian was shot in his vehicle as he was leaving the station in the early hours of the morning. A panic button was then pushed and a very clear message left for us to find. These are the similarities.'

'No script this time?' Price asked.

Helen raised tired eyes. 'No, no script, but a typed message was left on the windscreen, which is significant.' She looked down to her notebook. 'It appears to be the same size and font as the others and reads,' she balanced a slim pair of glasses on her nose and read, "Those that are tasked with me shall become my next task."'

'He knew?' Inspector Alison Moore sat opposite Price. Her voice was breathy, dramatic. 'He knew that Sergeant Cutter was leading the investigation? Am I reading that right?' She answered her own question, 'He must have done.'

'That's the working hypothesis at the moment, yes,' Helen said.

'How could he know?'

Helen stood up. They watched her pace the room. 'There is no way he could have known without inside knowledge of the investigation. Certainly no one outside this station would be aware that Cutter was in charge.' She stopped and turned back to face her audience around the table. 'The reason you have all been turned out of your beds and brought in here today is simple. You represent every police constable and sergeant that work in South

Lennokshire and have been part of this investigation, or were on duty yesterday, or could have *any* inkling that Ian Cutter would be leading the chase for our suspect. We need to be clear, the man *or* woman who has so far killed four of our staff in cold blood is either getting assistance from, or *is,* a police officer working under one of you.' She paused. Some of them exchanged shocked glances. No one offered any response. 'Your brief is very simple. Get out there today and get in among your people on the ground, in the offices, in the patrol cars. Get hold of your sergeants, any PCs that you know to be particularly influential, whatever you need to do. Go to the personnel files, remind yourself of any disgruntled officers and what they might be disgruntled about, while considering access to firearms, or potential associates with access. Whatever you think might be relevant and even what you don't. I don't believe for one second that an officer makes a decision to involve themselves in something like this lightly. This person ought to be damned obvious to us. Any questions?'

There was a stunned silence, and Price took in the horrified faces around him.

Helen softened her tone. 'And let's not forget that we all lost friends yesterday. There is going to be a lot of emotion out there today — anger, sadness and an awful lot of fear. We won't be sending any officers out to calls without first assessing them fully, and they will have a firearms chaperone as often as possible. I would rather we keep the suggestion of an insider to ourselves for now. We'll get together for another chat later in the day.' Allowing no time for questions, she brought the meeting to an end. There was a scraping of chairs and excited talk. Helen had to raise her voice to be heard over the sudden noise. 'And people! We are looking at the security of officers coming to and from work. We will be letting you know what we can do later in the day. Needless to say, we all need to be more vigilant than we have ever been. This person has just brought the threat right to our door.'

'Ross!' Helen called out towards Price. He was at the rear of the departing group of officers, keeping his head down, desperate for some time alone to think.

'Ma'am?'

Helen waited until the last officer had closed the door behind them. 'I need you to stay. I'll get us another coffee.'

Price watched her walk away. Her high heels clicked on the polished wood, and she looked every bit the strong woman who knew how to sustain an image. Price scratched his head.

Helen beckoned to him from the bar area. 'Actually, Ross, you might as well come in here. The chairs are better.'

Price followed her into a partitioned-off room full of soft furnishings, all positioned to focus on the bar at the far end of the room. The shutters were down at the bar now, but the coffee machine fuzzed, clicked and spat. Helen stood next to it. Price looked out through the window. Another scorching day.

'Ross, you may not know these two officers.' Helen turned back, holding a tray bearing four cups.

Price looked across to where she was heading, and for the first time noticed two figures sitting in a dark corner. The man closest to him rose to his feet and shot out his hand. It looked as big as a dinner tray to Price. His weak smile faltered slightly under the man's crushing grip.

'This is Sergeant Barry Lance. He is the tactical commander for Lennoxshire Police, based out of Greyharbour. His team specialises in armed interventions.' The men exchanged nods. 'And this is Inspector Andrew Manto from our Professional Standards Department.' This man's handshake seemed uncertain, his nod half-hearted.

'Nice to meet you both,' Price lied. He was always uncomfortable around the PSD — the police who policed the police. He could recall a couple of meetings in which

Andrew Manto had featured. He had once delivered a presentation to all the inspectors on how to effectively investigate your own staff. Price was left with the impression that he enjoyed his role a little too much. Price sat down and looked at his two colleagues, both intent on the business of sugaring and stirring their coffee. The rest of Barry Lance's body matched his enormous hands. His build looked natural, deriving more from his genes than the gym. He had short red hair and neatly trimmed beard in a darker brown. He appeared to be very comfortable in his own skin, a look reinforced by the casual navy blue 'Tactical Command' polo shirt, tucked into navy cargo trousers and ending in a pair of huge black boots. He wore an oversized diver's timepiece on one wrist and a "Help for Heroes" charity band on the other.

Beyond him, Manto sat forward to sip from his coffee cup, which he held in both hands. His face bore the half-sneer, half-smile that he had maintained for his entire presentation, and which had made him instantly and universally disliked. He had eyes that were just too close together and greying hair shorn close to his scalp, maybe in an effort to disguise the fact that he was balding from the crown.

'Ross, our colleagues here are assisting us with the shootings, or Operation Tuscan as it has now been designated.'

'Tuscan?'

'Don't ask. The person responsible for allocating the names is a fan of a certain sports car apparently. Anyway, as I said to the others, we think that our offender is being helped by someone inside the organisation. Or, in the very worst case the offender *is* one of our people. We've called in Barry and Andrew, neither of whom know many people down this way, to assist. We need you to make sure Andrew is up to speed with everything we have so far, everything that Ian and you have already done.'

'That won't take long.' Price realised what he had implied. 'I mean no disrespect to Ian, he couldn't have done any more than he did, but there's just nothing much to go on at the moment. It was early days. I knew it was just a matter of time before he started making progress, but it seems that time was something he just didn't have.' He shook his head.

'I know what you meant,' Helen said. 'Whatever you find, PSD will need to be kept informed. This investigation is going to need a lot of manpower. Use Andrew for whatever you need, I'm sure he won't mind doing some of the legwork.' Helen attempted a smile but it vanished quickly. 'You'll be based here for now and your security is my primary concern. We may look to house you somewhere else, but that is under an ongoing risk assessment.'

Price was adept at seeing through management spiel, and he knew this meant, "Lennokshire Police can't guarantee your safety but they'll give it a go."

'What about resources?' Price was aware that there was a considerable amount of legwork to be done, and they wouldn't be able to do it while the threat remained.

'You have a team of seven trained detectives. You will hopefully have a sergeant running the team once I can get one in, and we may look at a neighbouring force to supply this. That may take a little time, but I think it would be tough on the team to come in this morning and find Ian had been instantly replaced. You will also have just about anything else that you may need. Your team will be based here and will take their direction from you.'

Price pursed his lips. 'Seven detectives may not be enough to get someone through the door quickly. Is there any way you can lean on the force resource unit to get us some immediate help from elsewhere?' Price wondered if he might have overstepped the mark.

'I agree with you. There's a lot of work to be done and I've already had a conversation with the FRU. They have as many as twenty detectives ready to assist us, but I don't want any more than that while we don't have a handle on the threat. That might not be an issue for too long though.' Helen paused. 'You see, there have been some developments following Ian Cutter's death.' Her voice dropped to almost a whisper. 'We have a suspect.'

Price hadn't seen this coming. He narrowed his eyes and leaned forward. 'Really?'

'Yes. It seems Ian might have been responsible for a bit of a breakthrough after all.'

Price leaned further forward. 'Something he didn't tell me?'

'No, no, it's nothing like that. Ian's shooting followed the same basic MO as the previous ones but with a couple of significant differences.'

'Differences?'

'As Ian was leaving work, he didn't have his police radio on him. To be honest, he rarely carried it when he was at work either, but this gave the shooter a problem. He appears to have solved it by using his *own* personal radio. As you know, each radio is tailored to the person it was issued to, and our shooter left his at the scene. It appears he might have made a big mistake.'

Price's eyes opened wide. 'Who?'

'You will find out very soon, I can't divulge it right now but rest assured we have already started the ball rolling to get him in, and when we do, it will be you and Inspector Manto that will be questioning him. It's not about trust or lack of it, you understand, it's about protecting you. There's an intelligence officer sitting on the target right now. Let's just say that the name makes a lot of sense.'

'Makes sense?'

Helen nodded. 'From what we know about this person and from the evidence left at Cutter's murder, I'm certain it's our offender.'

'So why sit on him? Why don't we bring him in now?'

'I want him in but we need to do this right, and that's where Barry here comes in. We're waiting for his men to arrive. They will form a formidable arrest team. I want this done clean, I don't want anyone else hurt, and Barry is the man to do it.'

Barry Lance's smile contained no flicker of doubt.

'If all goes to plan, you will be in interview with our suspect by the end of the day and maybe we can all start getting some answers.'

'Excellent,' Price's said without conviction. 'You're sure this is the right man?'

Helen contorted her mouth into a sort of smile. 'Oh yes. This is our man.'

Price's mind filled with questions, like why would someone who is clearly organised enough to pull off four murders of high profile targets in a twelve-hour period, then go and make such a huge and basic error? He also wondered how the target would react to Barry Lance's team. If he was their man, he had already demonstrated his willingness to use extreme violence.

Price shook hands with Lance. Again, the crushing grip and the self-confident smile. Price made his way out of the place that a couple of months before had been the scene of Ian Cutter's retirement. He wondered whether the team tasked with the arrest was much concerned about ensuring that the target actually made it to an interview.

* * *

Helen Webb watched Price leave and then turned back to the two men. 'This needs to be clean, gentlemen, and it needs to be done right. If this isn't the answer I've got a team from the Counter Terrorist Unit on their way down. They report directly to the Home Office, and if they get a hold of this we'll all be out of the loop.' Helen scowled involuntarily. One thing she could not handle was losing control of her force.

Lance and Manto left the room and Helen went over to a top floor window. She had a good view out over the town, which from her lofty position and in the bright sunlight looked deceptively calm. Already she had received confirmed reports of looting on the high street, a spate of violent robberies in corner shops and numerous other opportunist attacks and crimes. The locals knew that the police would not be turning out for anything that wasn't life or death, and even when they did, the response would be four times slower than the previous week.

From up here Langthorne did not look anything like the smoking apocalypse of her imagination, but under the surface and away from her elevated position she knew that, for the time being at least, she had lost the town.

It was time to start taking it back.

CHAPTER 7

Barry Lance turned and addressed the man on his left and the two others sitting in the back of the Range Rover. 'He's on the move. He's in a vehicle, a 51 plate Ford Mondeo heading out of Langthorne. We have an unmarked chase car in behind him and two plain Volvos at point. He should hit the A259 in less than ten minutes and that's where we get our opportunity.' He and his team lived for jobs like these and the adrenalin was pumping through his veins.

His eyes flickered from man to man. 'We've got the go-to.'

The men in the vehicle knew this was firearms speak for loading and prepping their weapons. They headed for a quiet retirement cul-de-sac that had been chosen as being within a feasible distance for reaction. All four doors of the vehicle swung open. Four figures in plain black overalls put their steel-capped boots down on the tarmac and pulled their G36 assault rifles from the locked armoury. They manoeuvred these over their heads, snapping the ammunition into place, and then readied their secondary weapon, a matt-black Glock pistol, tugging and releasing the top slide to chamber a round before sliding them into their leg holsters. Two of the men checked a pouch on their ballistic vest which contained six-bangs. In an arrest situation the idea was to create so much noise and confusion that the target would have no idea what had hit him until he was in cuffs. Finally, each tugged a thick, black balaclava over his head and climbed back up into the Range Rover, where they were concealed behind darkened windows. The decision to dress like an armed gang rather than police officers was a tactical one — armed gangs don't play by the rules.

Over a designated and secure channel, Barry informed the other vehicles that they were on the move. He listened as two similarly equipped Volvos confirmed the go-to and then the chase car took up the commentary.

The Volvos quickly found their position, three cars behind the Land Rover Discovery chase car which was still providing running updates. This was a further two cars behind the target Mondeo. Four by fours were the vehicles of choice when conducting what was known as a "hard stop" on an armed target. Their elevated seating position made them effective for observing vehicles, and also provided a good position from which to fire on a moving target.

Lance was busy on the radio. He had four marked traffic units closing the roads where civilian vehicles would join the A259, along which the target car was proceeding. This was a long stretch of road that linked numerous seaside towns, including Hythe, where Patrol Sergeant Freddie Lee had been shot the day before. The road ran through the towns along the seafront, with the sea on the left. As it passed through villages and towns the speed limit dropped to 30 or 40 mph, but there were stretches where it opened up a little wider, where the only scenery was beach on one side and marshland on the other, and speeds could increase to 60 mph or more. One of these stretches had already been identified as the point where the pursuing cars would make their move. It was not far away now.

The traffic cars had confirmed their positions, road closures were in place, and a town suddenly gave way to sparse marshland. Lance barked, 'Strike!' The Range Rover lurched forward. Lance moved out across the central white line, the car pitching a little on its raised suspension, the big wheels scrabbling for traction among the loose stones and potholes littering the middle of the road. The Range Rover emerged from the row of traffic and began to overtake the first of eight cars that were between it and the target. Just as powerful, the Discovery in front of him responded in much the same way. The driver, aware of the impending strike, had eased back from the car in front but now made up the distance, relying on the road closures ahead as a blind corner approached. Lance was aware of the sound of car horns blaring as they sped past. The target car was now visible and it had increased its speed to 70 mph.

The Discovery radioed back. 'One white male occupant only. Repeat, one occupant, front seat driver. No weapons observed at this time. Male fits description.'

The Discovery accelerated forward past the Mondeo. They were now at the beginning of a long straight stretch of road, devoid of any other cars. After it swept past the target it jerked back across, cutting in front of the Mondeo, which reacted with a flicker of the brake lights. The Land Rover manoeuvred back out into the middle of the road and stayed there. A Volvo had also made its way into an overtake position behind Barry. He powered the Range Rover past the last car before the target, which reacted to the Volvo by dropping back. The Volvo at the rear cut into the line of traffic directly behind Barry, causing heavy braking and angry punching of horns. A figure wearing a balaclava in the rear of the Volvo waved the civilian cars back. The row of cars following the target fell back. The rear car of the strike team was now in front of the civilian cars. A police sign appeared in its rear window and the line of cars immediately started to slow.

The Mondeo had been isolated.

Barry floored the accelerator again, moving the Range Rover out where it could get alongside the Mondeo. Barry's vehicle was the first to open fire. An assault rifle spat several rounds through the rear window of the Mondeo, shattering it. The Mondeo braked and the Volvo responded by punching it twice from behind. The target increased his speed, but any attempt to accelerate away from the faster vehicles had to be futile. More rounds smashed into the side of the car, the rim around the driver's door sparked and rounds penetrated the roof above the passenger side at the front of the car. The Land Rover pulled back in front of the Mondeo, and stayed at a constant 60 mph. The Range Rover drove alongside. The rear occupant readied a six-bang, pulled the pin and threw. It fell through the shattered rear window of the Mondeo and bounced around on the seat. The lead car took its cue from this and hit the brakes. The target's attention was elsewhere and the impact into the back of the Land Rover was enough to inflate two of the Mondeo's airbags and damage a front wheel. It bucked to the right and bounced off the side of the Range Rover and veered left. Something came free from the underside of the Land Rover and made contact with the road, shooting sparks directly into the interior of the Mondeo. The driver applied the brakes hard, and the three wheels that still functioned locked up. It was trapped. It made contact with the Volvo behind for a third time and again with the chase car in front before Barry's Range Rover veered violently into its side. The Mondeo had nowhere to go and its stop was sudden, the nearside met solidly with the raised mud bank that lined the road. The airbags were already spent and the occupant was thrown forward into the steering wheel.

'Hands where I can see them, hands where I can fucking see them!' The order came from an officer inside the Range Rover that was still side-on, and was accompanied by two rounds fired into the steaming bonnet in front of the driver. 'Put them out of the window. On the right side. On the door, on the fucking door!'

A second six-bang hit the steering wheel of the Mondeo and bounced into the driver's lap. His hands disappeared back into the car as he batted it away. It finished its cycle on the floor, against the clutch pedal, and the driver lifted his legs up and hugged his knees. A man in a balaclava pointed his assault rifle through the broken windscreen and barked out, 'Hands on the door sill, hands on the fucking door sill!'

The Mondeo's driver did as he was told, but his right hand shot up as it came into contact with broken glass. A second armed man, also in a balaclava, appeared at the driver's window. He thrust his rifle through, pushing it hard into the target's right cheek, while another officer took hold of the seated man's hands, roughly smacking them against the driver's door sill where he held them down, ground into the glass.

The rifle jerked against the suspect's cheek. 'Move and I will blow your fucking head off. Do you understand?'

The man nodded slightly, eyes on the rifle at his cheek. Someone put the cuffs on too tightly and he winced. Someone else reached through the window, took hold of him by the top of his trousers and hauled him upwards and out through the driver's window. He fell hard against the tarmac, striking his forehead. He wriggled onto his side and was kicked in the ribs, causing him to cough up bile and white phlegm. A knee rested on the side of his face, pushing his cheek into the tiny shards of glass scattered over the road. Hands went through his pockets, searching him roughly. 'Jesus! Did you *piss* yourself?'

Laughing, the men stood around the trussed-up figure lying on the tarmac. One of them stamped hard on a hand. The suspect pulled his cuffed hands under his chin and brought up his knees in a foetal position. Another kicked at the stricken man's exposed torso. 'Don't you fucking look at me!'

Lance moved forward. 'Alright, lads! I gotta call the boss.' He lifted his phone to his ear. It only rang once.

'It's done?' Helen Webb breathed.

'It's done. He's in custody.'

'And it's definitely him?'

One of Lance's men took hold of the thick, blood-matted hair and lifted the face of their target. The man's eyes were half shut, and one was already swollen. Blood, dirt and grit littered the untidy beard that covered his face and neck. He wore a filthy shirt with a blood-stained collar and gave off a smell of piss-soaked trousers and alcohol. Lance unfolded a picture with the name and date of birth of the target printed underneath. The man in the picture was smiling, clean shaven, wearing a shirt and tie with the top button undone, a police identity card hanging round his neck, but Lance was sure. Underneath all the shit, it was definitely the right man.

'Yeah,' he said, and smiled, 'It's definitely him. It's definitely George Elms.'

CHAPTER 8

Police officers are often guilty of putting two and two together, matching people to a crime, without the bother of evidence gathering. So Detective Sergeant George Elms immediately made a lot of sense, even to people who might have previously called him a friend. Eighteen months ago he had been suspended after being involved in the shooting of a fellow officer. The chief constable himself had fallen that night, and no one had ever got to the bottom of what had actually happened.

News of his arrest reached Langthorne House police station long before the man was actually brought through the gates. He arrived in a marked cell van that lurched and rocked as it rode up the pavement, causing the occupant of the rear cage to slam against the cold metal. Jack Leslie had made it his business to be at the station for the return of the arrested man, and was waiting on the first floor when he heard the buzz that the van had pulled up at the back gate. He appeared outwardly calm as he stepped over to the window, parted the blinds and stared down as the van dock closed with a metallic clunk. Soon the prisoner would be escorted into the custody area.

'He's here,' Jack muttered, his throat dry, and he turned and walked towards the double doors that led to the stairs.

* * *

George Elms experienced little more than a sensation of hazy familiarity as he stepped down from the high lip at the rear of the vehicle. Rough hands on his shoulders pushed him forward. Concussion still fogged his mind and his senses, and the six-bangs had aggravated his tinnitus to the point where it almost completely blocked out anything external. He turned his face towards the sun that caught in the fine metal mesh, forming an orange backdrop to the millions of black spots in front of his eyes. His movements were slow, the officers held him firmly either side, as if leading an infant making their first steps. George's ears let through fragments of noise, the odd word, the sound of doors being slammed behind him. He felt as if he was walking underwater.

The hands on George's shoulders steadied him, and there were other hands under his arms. They brought him to a halt at a thick, metal door painted a heavy grey colour with a sliver of a porthole. He struggled to peer through and made out shadows, indistinct shapes. Someone shoved him hard in his back as the door swung open. His trousers were cold, damp and clammy round his thighs, his socks and shoes had been removed and his bare feet dragged on the floor.

George could make out the beginnings of a long ramp that sloped gently up to a high-sided desk. The padded rubber flooring was surprisingly springy underfoot and helped him to walk. He smelled air tainted with unwashed and sweaty bodies, and all of a sudden he knew exactly where he was. Langthorne's custody area opened up in front of him. The corridor was just wide enough for four people to stand across it shoulder to shoulder, then around six or seven metres in, it opened up into a much larger space. George was aware of figures to his left and right. Instinctively he kept his head bent forward, avoiding eye contact. He heard the voices though. They penetrated the white noise in his ears and some seemed familiar. He felt another couple of digs in his back and he was pushed forward to where a white-shirted sergeant stood tall behind the desk, facing him. He could sense people standing closer to him now, their breath on the back of his neck and the side of his face.

'Scum!'

'They're gonna fucking have you!' Someone threw a cup of water into his face. The contents spilled into his eyes and he gasped at the cold.

'Look at the state of 'im!'

'You're fucked now, George, fucked, mate!' A gob of spittle struck his neck.

The voices were growing in number. There was a scuffle to his right, someone was being restrained by four colleagues, shouting threats of violence and vengeance.

George received one last shove from behind and collided with the desk at chest height. His hands were now cuffed behind his back.

A jailor took up position next to him. He looked George up and down and then turned to the desk sergeant. 'He's got wet trousers, Sarge. I'll get him a paper suit.'

The sergeant looked down from the desk. 'No, Jim. Let him lie in it.'

A voice shouted from behind, 'Too fucking right!' Another paper cup missed its target, spilling drips on the desk and rolling to the floor. The voices grew louder. George couldn't distinguish that of anyone he knew. His head and face throbbed while his stomach was knotted, he was nauseous after the hard kicks, and it hurt to breathe. George lifted his damaged face towards the sergeant. It took all he had, but he managed a smile.

'Hello, Sergeant,' George said. 'Don't suppose I could get a drink?'

The custody sergeant was a tall man made taller by the raised floor on his side of the desk. He had to stoop to where George had rested his chin on its wooden surface. 'You'll get fuck all from me.'

A female voice rang out, silencing the custody area. 'Everybody out! Leave this man alone!' George rolled his head, and his eyes came to rest on a face he knew. The chief superintendent moved forward and stood next to him.

'Why is this man standing in wet clothes?'

The custody sergeant merely curled his lip.

'Get this man a change of clothes now!'

'Maybe we should get him a newspaper in the morning too?'

'We will afford him his human rights, just like we do every single person that walks, or is dragged through that door. Do you understand?' She sounded furious at his insubordination.

'Yeah. I mean, I just—'

'You will come and see me later with your explanation as to why this man has been subjected to such a disgraceful circus. Right now, you get him to somewhere he can sit down and you get him assessed by the custody nurse. Do you have any problems with that, Sergeant?'

'No, no, I'll get it done, ma'am.'

The jailor reappeared, rustling a blue paper suit with matching paper slippers.

'Jim, can you take this man to cell 4 please, and get him a drink. I'll call the nurse,' the sergeant said to him.

Jim began to lead George towards his cell. George heard Helen Webb call out, 'Hold on!' and they stopped to let her catch up. She reached into her pocket and produced a small handcuff key. She unfastened the cuffs from his wrists, which were slippery with blood. She nodded for the two men to continue, and Jim guided George into the cell. The door was already open and George became aware that Helen had followed them.

Jim announced that he was going to get a cup of water. George rubbed at his wrists and flexed his hands as he entered. He shuffled to the far corner and turned with his back against the wall. His legs gave way almost instantly. He made an untidy heap on the floor. His face and lip still leaked blood. One of his eyes was swollen shut. He was dirty and unshaven and he was aware that he stank.

'You look like shit, George,' Helen said.

Jim came back, still holding the paper suit and with a cup of water in his other hand. Helen took both items off him and he nodded and took his opportunity to leave. She stepped into the cell. Her heels clicked on the cold stone floor, and George lifted his eyes to the figure that stood above him. He smiled, but his eyes were opaque, lifeless. She bent and placed the water beside him, then hesitated, like she was building to say something more. A few seconds passed, she dropped the paper suit to the floor and walked out without looking back.

CHAPTER 9

The building had once been a paper mill. Helen Webb had been a visitor here on a couple of occasions when her primary school had run trips, and she felt a sudden nostalgia. The mill had been fully functioning then of course, and she could still smell the warm aroma of pulp that had emanated from the giant vats. A natural stream had run through the middle of the factory, channelled through the thick concrete floor. Stepping out of her car, Helen heard running water and saw that the stream was still there. It didn't run through the middle of the building anymore, the developers had seen fit to divert it around the outside into a feature for the luxury flats on the ground floor.

Sarah Elms lived in flat nine, down a long corridor that ran straight through the middle of the building. The door, like the others, was of highly polished pine. Helen made a fist and knocked.

Sarah Elms was shorter than Helen remembered. They had met at a formal dinner a couple of years ago. Helen had then seen her several times at the numerous hearings her husband attended after his suspension from

Lennokshire Police. The hearings had ended when the Crown Prosecution Service had offered no evidence against George, deciding that a prosecution was "not in the public interest." Lennokshire Police had convinced the Independent Police Complaints Commission that George Elms' actions eighteen months ago in the middle of the notorious "Effingell" Estate, had been in self-defence. Had he not acted as he did, they said, he would have ended up dead like Inspector Jacobs and the chief constable. Two people were known to have walked away alive from that incident. George Elms had never been called by the courts to answer for his part and the other had never been caught. Or pursued, for that matter. Helen had been instrumental in ensuring that the investigation came to its abrupt and unsatisfactory end.

After the formal hearings and investigations she had cut ties with the Elms family. George had remained suspended ever since. The official reason was that he suffered from tinnitus, which was so severe that it caused him confusion and concentration problems, balance issues, nausea and even blackouts. The worst effect, though, had been insomnia — George hardly slept at all. There was talk of post-traumatic stress disorder, but Lennokshire Police were keen to play this down. Helen had spent a lot of time and effort keeping a lid on the "George Elms problem," as she referred to it. She had never stopped to think how this might have affected the man himself. Now, having seen him sitting in a custody cell, stinking of alcohol and his own urine, she found herself wondering what life must have been like for his family, and how his wife would react when they met.

'Sarah!' Helen smiled.

Confused, uncertain eyes peered back out at her. 'What do you want?'

'I was hoping to talk to you.'

'I think we're done with talking, don't you?' Sarah pushed the door shut.

Helen was tempted to stick out a foot to stop it but didn't want to act aggressively so soon. Instead she called out, 'George has been arrested.' She stepped closer to the door and waited. 'For murder.'

The door clicked open. 'You've got five minutes,' Sarah said.

The apartment had no hallway, and Helen followed Sarah straight into a large kitchen-diner. Double doors beyond it opened onto a balcony that overhung the running stream. One of the kitchen walls had a large wooden board with numerous certificates pinned to it with brightly coloured pins. They had been awarded to Charley Elms for "best pupil," "best story" and "best in class," among other achievements. Sarah leaned against the kitchen units and crossed her arms, looking at Helen.

'Are you and George still in touch?' Helen asked.

'What's that got to do with you or anyone else?' Sarah barked, and tossed her dark hair.

So that was how it was. 'When did you see him last?'

'Why has he been arrested? After all this time, all he's been through! You told us you were done with him, and he wasn't facing any criminal charges.'

Helen stepped back a pace. 'That was true. We had every intention of leaving your husband alone, Sarah. Unfortunately it seems that he had no such intention towards us.'

'What do you mean?'

'Yesterday, four police officers were shot. Separate incidents, but we believe the same person was responsible. That person showed an in-depth knowledge of the police and how we function, and demonstrated his ability with a firearm. I have never seen such hatred for the police.' Helen watched Sarah's face contort in confusion.

'You think George shot police officers? What police officers?'

'There's good evidence, evidence that clearly links him to the scenes. It's early in the investigation but he certainly has some questions to answer.'

'Questions to answer? Have you seen him recently?' Sarah's voice cracked.

'Today. For the first time in a long while.'

'He looks like shit, doesn't he? You know he's been drinking?'

'I worked it out.'

Sarah forced a laugh. 'You worked it out? From what? The state of him? The smell? Have you seen his flat? He's a proud man, George, and look what you lot did to him!'

Helen sighed. 'Sarah, all we did was keep him out of prison, and don't think that was easy after what he did that night.'

'Don't you come here and tell me that you did my husband any favours! Don't you dare,' said Sarah.

Helen was silent.

'After the explosion at our home, and the shooting, it was impossible to just go back to normal. The insurance company put us in a hotel and offered to rebuild the place, but we couldn't go back there, not after that. Our family home was gone and George, well he just had no desire to look for another. His tinnitus has been a real battle. He just doesn't sleep with it, and he has to leave rooms with certain noises, and on bad days he can just black out altogether.' Sarah looked up at Helen. Her eyes were red and full of tears. 'He started drinking, just to try and sleep at first. He was being questioned daily by you people, sometimes for four, five hours at a time without a break, and he knew that if he said the wrong thing he would go to prison. He was terrified of that. He did his best to be normal around Charley but she knew something was up, and that broke his heart. His drinking got worse. He went from using it to get to sleep to using it just to get through the day.'

'It must have been difficult for you,' Helen said.

'It became impossible. We both knew that it was affecting Charley so we agreed that George would move out for a while, just to get himself off the drink and get his head together. When the word came back from you lot that he was in the clear, I thought he might be able to beat it, but it didn't happen. You wouldn't let him come back to work, so he was at home on his own all day with nothing to do but self-medicate.'

'People got hurt, Sarah. We couldn't just let him come back to pick up where he left off. He was due to be assessed to find out whether he could return. I'm sure you understand that we couldn't have him back until that was done.'

Sarah shook her head. 'I do, but you put that assessment back three times. George would build himself up for it, he wouldn't touch a drop in the days leading up to it, he practised what he needed to say, and then you would cancel, and he would . . . he would hit it so hard, I started to think he would never stop.'

'George must be upset about how it all worked out. I know he feels that Lennokshire Police have wronged him. I know he thinks he deserves more from a force that he put more than fifteen years' hard slog into.' Helen stopped and waited for the reaction.

Sarah's voice was low, anger bubbling under the surface. 'I know what you're suggesting. But he wouldn't do that. Sure, he felt let down by you lot, but he wouldn't shoot anyone.'

'Well, now we know that isn't true, don't we?' Helen chanced.

Sarah's reply was forced through gritted teeth. 'We've done this to death. George acted in self-defence that night, and it was accepted by your independent people. They grilled him and grilled him. He told them the same story time and time again, and you never wore him down, you never made him trip himself up, because he was telling the truth. And let's not forget that he wouldn't have had to take any action if any of you people had known what was going on right under your own noses. You lost control, and when he opened your eyes and gave you the name of the person responsible, you ignored it, buried your heads in the sand and hoped that it would all just go away to make sure you saved your own damned careers.' She sniffed. 'And it probably did — for you.'

'Sarah, I know how difficult it must have been for you. I know you went through it just as much as he did, but you have to believe me when I say that I did all that I could to keep George from answering for his actions in a court of law. If he had stood up in front of a jury there would have been no way of controlling the outcome and he may well have been sent to prison. For a very long time.'

Sarah had composed herself. 'You make it sound like you fought for George. We're not stupid. You all fought for yourselves and your reputations. What happened to George didn't matter to you, he was just a nuisance and if he'd gone down you might have gone with him.' Sarah stared at Helen, who avoided her eyes. 'Be honest, it would have been better for you if George had died that night too.'

Helen didn't answer.

'Wouldn't it?' Sarah persisted.

'George is in trouble now. I came here because I thought you would want to know. I shouldn't have come.' Helen turned towards the door.

'What evidence do you have against George? I bet there's nothing at all! You just thought you'd arrest him because of his past,' Sarah shouted after her.

Helen turned, slowly. 'He has shown himself capable of taking a man's life, Sarah. Neither of us can deny that. You say it was self-defence, and that may well have been the case eighteen months ago, but yesterday four people were shot *and killed* in cold blood. I'll spare you the details but I can assure you it was a display of pure hatred towards the police. There is good evidence, enough to bring George in and for him to have to answer some very difficult questions. If you know anything, anything at all that might shed some light on this, you have to let me know. There are four families out there suddenly having to come to terms with the fact that their dad, their husband, and even a grandmother won't ever be coming home from work. We have to make sure there are no more.'

'George wouldn't hurt anyone without good reason. He only hurt those men when they threatened us.'

Helen looked at Sarah, directly now. 'What about Paul Bearn?'

'I don't think any of us can really understand the sort of pressures George was under that night, the sort of fear he felt, but we all know that any choices he made came from the right place. He was protecting himself and he's been trying to do the same ever since. If you've seen him you know he's not the man he was. George is a mess.' Sarah's tone held sadness and acceptance.

'He's a different man from the one I knew, you're right there. Maybe neither of us knows what he's capable of anymore.'

Sarah pushed past Helen and opened the door. 'I think you should leave.'

Helen stopped in the doorway and turned. 'If you remember anything that you think is relevant you'll let me know, won't you? Or if not me, someone at the station. You can call anonymously if you'd rather. We might have to release George while the investigation continues, and you might be able to stop any other officers from coming to harm.'

Sarah did not respond.

'Think about it,' Helen said, and stepped through the door.

* * *

Sarah Elms leaned against the door. She felt drained, exhausted. She was so tired of worrying, wondering. She walked back into the kitchen and picked up her mobile phone.

'Sarah, hey.'

'Sam, I'm so sorry to call. I didn't know who else I could speak to. Is it true about George? Do you know anything about it?'

Detective Constable Samantha Robins sighed. 'Listen, Sarah. I can't speak to you right now. I'm at the station. I'll call you in a bit, maybe we can meet up. Is that okay?'

'Thank you, Sam.'

* * *

Sam instantly wished she hadn't agreed to her part in this at all. She looked up at Andrew Manto, the inspector of Lennokshire's Professional Standards Department, who sat perched and attentive, on her desk.

He nodded. 'Perfect timing! Well done, Sam. Part one all sewn up.'

CHAPTER 10

A single cloud crept across the sun. It glowed white hot round the edges as if it had been branded in the sky. It passed, and the sun was once again unleashed.

One man had barely noticed the intense heat. He was leaning forward with his back towards the sun. He reached out, snatched up an empty crisp packet and scrunched it into a ball. A bumblebee bounced clumsily off a large yellow rose petal. Roses had been his mum's favourite. He stretched out a hand and touched the slab of granite, running his finger along the lettering that formed the name, 'Anne Forley.' Underneath the dates of her existence, was written, 'Daughter, wife, mother, missed.' He had chosen the words himself. They were deliberately concise and orderly, whereas the last few months of her life had been anything but.

'All right, lad?' The gardener smiled at him from a kindly, wrinkled face. 'Yours is always the prettiest.'

'There was litter,' grunted the man and stood up to face the gardener. He thrust out a hand and opened it to reveal the crisp packet.

The gardener shrugged. 'Kids. They have no respect. I can't be here all the time.'

The man cocked his head, running the notion through his head. 'Respect? Maybe you should teach them a little.' His eyes bored into the gardener, who picked up his rake and backed away slightly.

'If I see them I'll be sure to tell them. I'll leave you on your own then, son. These are personal moments.' The gardener turned away.

For an old man, the gardener moved easily. His shirt had grass cuttings on it and there was a sweat patch on his back. He swung the rake out in front of him and let it bump the ground as he walked. He started a tuneless whistle.

The man curled his lip in a sneer, and set off after him, with his fists balled. 'Respect!' He came up behind the gardener and swung his fist hard at the back of the old man's head, connecting with the softer part. The gardener collapsed on the grass, head down. The man stood over him, his chest rising and falling, anger and adrenalin pumping round his body. The gardener twitched on the ground. The man looked at the rake, lying a few inches away.

He picked it up and ran it through his hands. He felt the handle end of the rake, it was smoothed to a rounded tip. The gardener stirred again. He muttered something and his eyes fluttered open. He stared at the figure standing over him. The man squatted and grasped the back of the gardener's head. He gripped the rake, turning it so that the tip pointed towards the gardener. '*If* you see them? You don't care about them and you don't care about her.' He pushed the end into the gardener's eye and the old man screamed. The handle plunged through the eye and then hit something denser.

The gardener was silent now.

CHAPTER 11

'Well, this was a little unexpected,' Helen Webb said.

Her voice echoed off the stone walls. George Elms tried to open his eye and winced. His concussion had worn off and now he could do with a drink. The tinnitus was loud in his ears, whooshing and whistling as if someone was trying to tune in an old radio.

George was lying on his side on the floor. The paper suit still lay where it had been dropped a few hours earlier. He had vomited, and his mouth was dry and tasted of blood. His trousers were stiff with dried urine. The bottoms had scorch marks from the six-bang grenades.

George squinted up at Helen Webb. 'Which bit?'

Instead of answering, Helen said, 'Can I get you anything?'

George winced again. 'I think you've done enough for me, thanks.' His hand moved to touch his ribs. 'I see the tactical teams have lost none of their enthusiasm.'

'We couldn't take any risks. It seems you've become a very dangerous man, George.'

He expelled air in a laugh that made him wince again, and his hand rested on his ribs. 'A dangerous man? Do I look like a dangerous man to you?'

'We both know that it can be very difficult to say what a dangerous man looks like. We tend to go on the evidence.'

'And what exactly do you have evidence of?'

Helen stepped into the cell, her hands on her hips. 'George, this may not have registered when it was said to you out on the street, but you are under arrest for the murder of four members of my police staff in the last twenty-four hours.'

George looked up. His one good eye widened. Through the tinnitus, he had had to really concentrate to take in her words. His own smell seemed worse than ever.

Helen's expression was one of disgust. 'You were also arrested for drink-driving. Seems you were some way over the limit. We're waiting on the results to see just how far.'

George was somehow able to muster a smile. 'I don't recall being read my rights, being asked about a solicitor.'

Helen shifted the hands on her hips in a shrug. 'Do you want a solicitor?'

George tried to reach for the paper suit and groaned. 'Well, I'd fucking say so, wouldn't you? I mean I could lose my driving licence here!' He held the suit to his chest. 'And I need a shower.'

* * *

Helen Webb slammed the door to the custody office. The custody sergeant was eating a banana and the jailor was sitting with his feet up, watching the monitor showing George's cell. The occupant lay on the floor with his arms crossed over his chest, as if lying in a coffin.

'What did he say?' asked the jailor.

'He wants a shower,' Helen said.

'Anything else? Does he know what he's here for now?'

Helen ignored the question. She stared hard at the jailor, who still had his feet up and had now opened a bag of crisps. 'I *said*, he wants a shower.'

The jailor finally stood up.

'The sooner he has a shower and a change, the sooner we can get him into an interview, and maybe get some answers.'

The jailor gave a curt nod and hurried out of the office.

'And, Sergeant, can we arrange for a solicitor please, as soon as possible?' She spun on her heels and made her way out of the custody area and back into the belly of the station.

* * *

'Sergeant Elms,' the jailor said.

The door had swung open and another visitor stood blocking the light from the corridor. From his position on the floor, George made out the rotund and smiling form of a former colleague.

George struggled to sit up. 'Jim the jailor. Just "George" from now on, mate.' He ran a hand through his matted hair, then down to his face, to try and assess the areas that were swollen and throbbing.

'Yeah, I heard you were in a bit of trouble.'

George gave a laugh that worsened the throbbing in the side of his face. Talk about stating the obvious.

'I don't believe it though, mate.'

George thought he sounded uncertain. 'You're not in charge of the investigation, are you, Jim?'

'No, mate, I'm just here to bring you a tea.' Jim lifted a steaming mug.

'Well, that's a shame then.'

'It's proper tea though, none of that machine rubbish. I made it in the kitchen with my own tea bags.'

George's smile was sincere, despite the way it hurt his face. He'd always got on okay with Jim. Their relationship consisted of nothing more than small talk and a bit of banter, but Jim was always genuine. He struck George as being keen to please. He was overweight and his head was shaved close to his scalp.

'And a proper mug, too,' George added.

'Yeah. I'll have to stay with you while you drink it, mate, so I can take it away when you're done.'

George reached for the mug. 'Ah, yes. So I don't do myself any harm.'

'You know how it all works, Sarge — Sorry, George.'

George raised the mug as if in a toast. 'Certainly I do.' Then he looked intently at his jailor. 'Imagine, Jim, that you live a full life. You have a family, a job and you have, well, happiness.'

Jim cocked his head slightly, listening.

'Imagine you have all that and then it suddenly all falls apart to the point where you're sat in a prison cell in piss-soaked trousers, with sick in your beard and blood in your mouth, suffering from a hangover from three weeks' solid drunk.'

Jim's eyes widened.

'Imagine you've got to that point, a disgrace for anyone, let alone a proud man who once respected himself and his place in society. Do you think, Jim, that a man going through all of that, who might just have reached rock bottom, the lowest of the low, do you think a man like that would consider taking the final step, bringing on the total humiliation of ending it all, showing he couldn't take it,' George took a swig of the tea, 'With a sharpened piece of a *teacup*?' George finally gave way and exploded in hysterical laughter.

And before the custody sergeant could make it to the door to see what the noise was all about, Jim the jailor had very much joined in.

CHAPTER 12

Detective Constable Samantha Robins was very uncomfortable. She had not been bothered by the summons from a senior officer from the Professional Standards Department. She was long past the point in her career when this made her flustered. Her discomfort was caused by the way the PSD representative was looking at her, and the tone of his voice. In short, he was leering.

Inspector Andrew Manto was leaning back in his chair, his knees touching the underside of the table. He was a tall man in his early forties with thinning, brown hair. He wore loud red braces that stood out against his blue-checked shirt. Sam was in a long black skirt that finished high on her body, tied with a wide belt. She raised a hand to push back her hair and became aware that the inspector was staring at her bust.

'Now, Sam. I know the PSD have a reputation among *the norms*,' he made quotation marks in the air with his fingers. 'But what you have to understand is that we're not here to catch you out. We don't want to upset the good cops.' His laugh sounded false. 'What we want is to let the good cops do their job *without* the worry of the bad cops.'

The inspector leaned back and put his thumbs under his braces. 'Does that make sense to you?'

Sam had been given the PSD talk as part of her initial training, and numerous times since then, during the aftermath of the chief constable's death eighteen months ago. She'd heard it all before and each time, it seemed to become more patronising.

Sam did her best to sound disinterested. 'Sure.'

'You need to feel like you can talk freely and comfortably to me. Do you feel comfortable, Sam?'

The inspector sat up, leaned towards Sam, reached out a hand and went to place it on top of hers. She snatched it away.

'What do you need?' she said.

Manto smiled. 'That's the attitude. George Elms, it appears, is one of the *bad* cops, Sam, someone the likes of me and you should be worried about. All the good, hard work and effort that you put into your career can be undone by someone like that. You can become tarnished with the same reputation that he has. Do you understand what I'm saying?'

Sam crossed her arms. 'I don't see him as a bad anything.' She had been interviewed at length by PSD with regard to her relationship with George Elms. They'd asked what she had observed about him, what he had said to her, how he conducted himself around her, and they had made it quite clear throughout that it would be good for her career if she came up with something, anything, as long as it was damaging. Sam had never changed her stance. She supported her sergeant. He was a good man and he had been good to her.

The inspector stood up abruptly and shook his head. 'I see. You're aware that George is in custody facing allegations that he shot and killed four members of the police family? Four of *us*, Sam.'

Sam nodded. 'One thing I've learned since I started in this job is how easy it is to get arrested, especially when there's a murder. Anyone linked to anything to do with a murder will get nicked. The fact that he's here doesn't mean he's guilty.'

The inspector pursed his lips. 'No. You could well be right, but suppose he did shoot those people? As police officers, *investigative* police officers no less, we have to investigate him fully. That might show he's guilty or of course, it might prove he is not.'

Sam didn't react.

'We need to know a bit of background about George. I have spoken to people that knew him, they say that he's a changed man, and we need to understand what form that change has taken. We need to find out if he feels resentment, bitterness towards Lennokshire Police, to the sort of level where he might commit the type of crimes that we have seen over the last few days. We also need to know if he's done anything that might suggest he was preparing for it.'

Sam sighed. 'And you need me to help by talking to him?'

He beamed. 'No flies on you, are there? We may well be forced to bail him once he's been interviewed here at the police station, and for all we know he has more unspeakable acts planned for his release. You have a relationship with him, Sam. Maybe you can get a little bit of a view of his state of mind. You never know what he might divulge to someone he trusts.'

'It's not like we're the best of friends. I'm not his confidante. I've barely spoken to the man in eighteen months. He's not sought me out to reveal his dark secrets during that time, so why would he now?' This wasn't quite true. Sam and George had been in infrequent contact over the last eighteen months, but it had trailed off to almost nothing.

'Well, that might be the case, but George is a proud man and I wouldn't necessarily expect him to go out confiding in people, asking for their opinions or their help.

But, if he were to be contacted by a friendly voice? Someone on his side, as it were, he just might give a snippet, something that could help us save lives.'

Sam looked up. 'A voice?'

'Of course. We're not asking you to visit the man in person. We don't want to be putting you in harm's way, Sam, now do we?'

'So you want me to call him?'

'That's all, and I'd like you to use this phone, just so there are no security issues. Also it gives us direct contact — a hotline to each other if you will.'

Sam picked up the new-looking Blackberry mobile phone that he pulled out of a drawer and slid over to her. She wasn't naïve, she knew it would have something on it, either a listening device or a simple tracker, or both. She saw her opportunity to leave and decided against arguing with this man. She stood up, with the parting words, 'I'll give it some thought.' She checked the new mobile phone was switched off and dropped it in her bag.

As she left, Ross Price rapped on the door and entered.

CHAPTER 13

The interview team sent to formally question George Elms entered Langthorne custody area at 08.12 hours on the last day of June. The temperature was already uncomfortably hot. The custody area lacked ventilation, and the warm air was redolent with the odour of unwashed bodies, stale alcohol and urine.

George didn't sleep well at the best of times, but in the muggy heat, amid the slamming of doors, bright lights and occasional shouting of other prisoners, he had not slept at all. At least he looked and smelled better, having managed some sort of a shave, and he was freshly showered and changed into the paper suit. He had looked in the shower room mirror and seen that the suit, combined with his battered face, made him look every bit the convicted criminal. His clothes had been taken away for forensic investigation. They would be prodded, tested, and inspected for the slightest link to the scenes, the victims, or the weapon that had fired the fatal shots. He had been informed that his home address had been searched too, along with his bullet-ridden car. He knew the process well, they hadn't needed to tell him.

Police interviews were a game, which the interviewing officers and defence solicitors played out in full awareness of what they were doing. The prisoner would also play their part, usually unaware of the rules. This prisoner, however, knew very well how the game was played. The solicitor representing George was Howard Staples, a man so large he needed to duck under the doorways in the custody area. He had spent twenty-eight years as a police officer, retiring as a sergeant. He knew the process inside and out, he knew the rules of the game and how to manipulate them. He also knew that, no matter what the evidence or the seriousness of the allegation, the odds would generally be stacked in favour of his client.

* * *

Howard had spent forty minutes in the custody area with Inspector Price, before meeting with George. This was the first part of the game: disclosure. The police made the legal advisor aware of why their client had been arrested, some or all of the evidence they had, and what outcome they were looking for, even at this early stage. During this meeting agreements were often reached, with talk of leniency for a confession. There had been no such offer this time. Howard left the meeting already aware that the case against George was as much personal as legal.

Howard then asked to see his client before the interview commenced.

George shuffled in. Howard extended his hand. 'I won't bother asking how you are.' Howard had met George only occasionally, since he had spent much of his police career in Special Branch, a department kept away from the day to day policing.

'I've been better. Have you had disclosure?' George asked.

Howard smiled. 'I have, and I'll be honest, George, they don't seem to have very much at all.' He took a seat opposite his client. His leather case had barely been used and he struggled with the single catch. Howard had brought in coffee in small plastic cups and offered one to George.

George grimaced. 'Definitely not. It's a desperate day when I start drinking custody coffee.'

Howard opened his notebook. 'First off, are you fit for interview? Because, bearing in mind what they have you in here for, if you're not on the button today, then I can make sure that—'

George cut in. 'No. I'm fine.'

Howard gestured at George's swollen face. 'All that from the arrest?'

George chuckled. 'Yeah, I think they're pissed off. You should see the state of my car!'

'You want me to make a representation about the use of force on arrest?'

George shook his head. 'I'm pretty sure that wouldn't get me very far, thanks.'

Howard took a long breath and fidgeted with his pen and notebook. 'So,' he said, 'What do you want to tell me about why we're both here today?'

'Well, I didn't shoot anyone if that's what you're getting at.'

'I'd like to know where we stand from the start, George. You know I have to ask.'

George nodded. 'I do. As yet no one's told me what this is all about. I don't know who the hell got shot, but it's no surprise I'm in line for it. It would suit a lot of people here if I just went away. Out of sight, out of mind.'

'Well, the evidence they have is frankly appalling. We'll get the interview done and unless they suddenly pluck something out of their arses, there will be no reason to keep you here. I will oppose any attempt at an extension and they certainly won't have enough to charge you with, so remand is not an issue. My advice, at this stage, based on the flimsy evidence they have, is to answer all questions with a succinct, "no comment." That way you do nothing to further their case, you give them no relevant lines of enquiry to go and check out, and consequently no reason to hold you here any longer.'

'No comment is as good as an admission of guilt though, if it ever gets to court.'

Howard smiled again. 'In some cases, sure. But you've been beaten up. You're confused about the whole thing and you have no idea why you've been arrested, so you don't want to say anything that might incriminate yourself until you are aware of the full facts. That sounds reasonable to me and I'm sure it would to a jury of your peers.'

'I'm happy to answer their questions,' George said. 'I've not left my flat for nigh on two weeks. Most of that time I was in a drunken stupor and the rest I was asleep. What possible evidence do they have linking me to any scene?'

Howard studied his notebook. 'It is alleged that an item was found at one of the scenes that can be attributed to you.'

'An item? What item?'

'They didn't disclose that, but they must be pretty certain it can only have been left by you.'

'Not a forensic link then? An actual *thing*?'

'A physical object, I was led to believe, with possible forensics of course, and that's about it. The rest is circumstantial, based on your past use of firearms, your resentment of the police and your close proximity to one or all of the incidents. They weren't really playing the disclosure game, I'm afraid. We'll just have to see what they come out with in interview.'

George stared at him. 'Close proximity?'

'You live in the same town. I would say it's as tenuous as that.'

George sighed and sat back. 'Let's do it. And I will have that coffee after all.'

* * *

At 09.25 hours the two-man interview team made themselves comfortable opposite the seated prisoner. Howard had moved round to sit beside George, and the game commenced with the two officers making a show of walking into the room with two boxes of exhibits. Inspector Price positioned himself a little further back than his colleague, to make it clear who would be leading the questioning. Andrew Manto read from a piece of paper without raising his eyes. 'George Alan Elms?'

George made no response.

'You know why you're here?' Manto peered over the top of the paper.

George returned the look. 'I know why I was arrested. Your boss popped in earlier to tell me.'

Manto nodded. 'You will know Inspector Price here, I assume?' George offered no response so Manto carried on, 'You will not know me. However—'

'I know who you are,' George cut in. 'You're PSD. I've seen plenty of you over the past year or so. You all carry yourselves the same way, like you're better than everyone else.'

Manto merely nodded. 'Well, good then. And you'll know that I have to formally identify myself for the DVD. My name is Detective Inspector Andrew Manto of the Professional Standards Department. I normally work at headquarters but I'm at Langthorne House today to conduct an interview under caution of George Elms, who was arrested for driving offences and four separate allegations of murder.' Manto paused and raised his eyes to the cameras pointing down from two corners of the room. 'This conversation will centre around the murder investigation.' Manto appeared to be enjoying himself.

The room itself was almost empty. It contained a solid white table and the chair George sat upon was bolted to the floor. A DVD recorder was positioned behind the two police officers, displaying the interview room filmed from above.

All the men announced their name and purpose, and the caution and other formal matters were read out to the prisoner. Then Manto assumed a pained expression and started the questioning.

George had braced himself. His recent experience with PSD had worn him out. The constant repetition was exhausting, going over and over the same ground, giving the same answers to the same questions. George made a conscious effort to calm himself. He stared at Manto, who was reading through his notes. Manto leaned on his elbows and brought his hands together under his chin.

'So, George,' he began, 'I want to start by talking to you about how you've been coping with your suspension. How have you been occupying the time?'

'I want to talk about the reason I'm here,' George said. 'The sooner you get onto that, the sooner I can go home. This interview is about something I'm supposed to have done, not how I've been.'

Manto pushed himself away from the table and crossed his arms. 'You're accused of shooting and killing four police staff in cold blood, George. You don't think that your mental state might be relevant to the investigation?'

'I didn't shoot anyone. So it isn't relevant, no.'

'Well, actually, we know that you did, don't we?' Manto watched George intently.

George was done defending himself for any past actions, and he was damned if he was going to go through it all again. 'I didn't kill those people.'

'And what people are those, George?'

'You tell me. I don't know anything about what's been going on with you lot. I keep my head down these days.'

Manto underlined something in his notes with a chewed biro. 'Are you alcohol dependent, George?'

'No.'

'You were drunk at the wheel. We don't have the results yet, but I'm confident they'll be positive.'

'I didn't shoot those people. That's what this is about, not about drink-driving.'

Howard cut in. 'You stated that this interview was to discuss the offence of murder. If you wish to talk about my client's alleged inebriation while driving a motor vehicle, then I will have to call for a break in proceedings. I have not yet discussed this offence with him, nor did you mention it in our disclosure.'

Manto went ahead with another question. 'Where were you going, George? Mid-afternoon and already drunk, where were you driving?'

Howard cut in for a second time. 'You will grant us a break if you insist on continuing to talk about the drink-drive offence.' He turned to George. 'I'll remind you that you don't have to answer any of these questions, George, especially if they're not relevant.'

Manto hadn't moved his eyes from George's face, and the prisoner stared back. 'You don't drink-drive, George, not a man like you, so what was so important?'

'I was going to see my family.' George immediately regretted his words. He didn't want to talk about his family.

Manto flipped through his notes. 'Your wife Sarah and daughter Charley?'

'Yes.'

'Did they know you were going to see them?'

'We'd talked about it. They were at a beach party.'

'My understanding was that your wife was having little or nothing to do with you. We've had a number of incidents, particularly over the past few months, where police have been called to your wife's place and have had to move you along. Apparently she's asked for our help and advice to get something formal in place to stop you just turning up.' Manto turned over more papers underneath his notebook. George recognised the format of intelligence reports. Manto removed one of them. 'This one particularly. She states here that you have a drink problem and that you'd turned up drunk when you were supposed to be taking your daughter out. Sarah refused to let you take her and she has now stopped you visiting at all.' Manto looked up. 'Says here she is considering applying for a judge's order blocking any contact from you except through a solicitor. It takes a lot for someone to get to that point, does it not?'

'I needed to speak to her. I just needed to see Charley, even if it was only for a few minutes.'

'Drunk?'

Howard moved his arm so that it rested against George. 'None of this is relevant. George has basic human rights, Inspector, just like we all do. I'm sure I don't need to remind you of his right to a private life, article eight, or his right to a family life, article twelve. The police are very much governed by the Human Rights Act are they not?'

'Let's talk about the right to life. Article two, I believe.' Manto nodded at Price.

Price reached down and picked out four papers from the box he had carried in and placed at his feet. He passed them to Manto, who laid them out side by side on the table. Manto sighed and seemed to hesitate. Then he turned over the first sheet, a colour photograph.

Police Constable Matthew Riley lay on his back, one arm stretched out beside his body, the other across his chest, holding down a piece of paper that showed stark white against the blood from the wound at the centre of his chest.

George leaned towards the image a little. He could see that the blood pooled round him was a darker shade of red than normal. He knew this to be a sign of an arterial bleed, something he'd seen before too many times. It would be thick and sticky with even a skin on top where it had started to congeal — like red boiled milk. Matthew's eyes were wide open. His open mouth looked as if he were still screaming.

There were no questions. Manto flipped over the second picture in silence.

PCSO Jan Thomas lay on a wooden floor. This time the photo was taken from a little further away and it was lit by sunlight, instead of a flash. It was a strange scene, peaceful almost. Shafts of sunlight came through the large windows of the sports hall. The body was slightly to the right of the frame, showing how close it was to the double doors, which had a metal bar across them with "push to exit" written in reflective green. There were drag marks left by the hard backs of PCSO Thomas's shoes. Again, a piece of paper rested on top of the body.

Watched closely by Manto and Price, George studied both images, but in the detached manner of a police officer on an investigation.

Manto flipped over the third picture and George started slightly as he looked down at Sergeant Lee. He lay with his legs still wrapped around his motorcycle. There was less blood in this picture, it had been contained beneath his riding leathers. George recognised him, he didn't know him well but he knew who he was.

Manto's hand rested on the final image. He looked up at George and flipped it over. Now George gave a sharp intake of breath. Ian Cutter didn't look much like the sarcastic, dry-witted old fossil that George had admired so much. Cutter was a very good detective, he had been protective of his team, and was well liked. Ian had a spark about him, he was sharp. There was nothing left of that in this photo.

Taken through the car window, the photo showed Ian sitting back in the driver's seat, his right arm hanging down at his side and his face turned to the camera. Ian's eyes were wide open. His skin was washed out and looked clammy, his lips were violet, and his mouth hung open. Cutter was wearing a white shirt, the middle of which was soaked in blood.

There was a long silence. George looked down at Ian Cutter sitting in his car. He knew the room was waiting for his reaction. 'He was a good guy. I thought he would have retired by now.'

Price immediately cut in, sounding angry. 'He did. But then he came back, seems he missed it.'

Manto nodded at Price, who again reached into the box at his feet. He passed across something that looked like a large mobile phone, tightly sealed in a bag marked, "Police Evidence."

'Do you recognise this?' Manto held it out to George. There were specks of what looked like dried blood on it.

'Of course. It's a police radio.'

'Can you be more specific?'

'Well, not really. It's just a police radio, and everyone out there in a uniform has one strapped to their chest or on their belt.'

'This radio was found at the scene,' Manto said. 'You see, our killer has been trying to get a message across. Each of these,' Manto swept his hand across the photos, 'Were accompanied by a press of the officer's panic button. The killer wanted every officer in Langthorne to be able to hear the moment when their colleague died.'

George waited, impassive.

'When Sergeant Cutter here was shot, it seems the killer had a problem. You see, Ian was a bit old school, he never really took his radio out with him when he was working, and when he was shot he was leaving for home, so it was sat in its charging cradle up in the nick. The killer still wanted his message to be heard, so we believe he used his own, personal issue police radio. And in his rush to get away from the scene after the shooting, he left it behind.' Manto paused. 'This radio is yours, George. You left it there after you shot him.'

George reacted with a grin that took a few seconds to form. 'That's all you have that links me to any of this? Just that? You've got fuck all! I would question whether you have *reasonable* suspicion to even arrest me! But you bring me through them fucking doors to be abused by staff who are out of control. And let's not forget you have authority to use *reasonable* fucking force as part of an arrest. Well, does this look reasonable to you?' George pointed his thumbs at his swollen face. The whooshing in his ears was loud now, and he couldn't make out Howard's words as he tried to communicate with him. 'Did you see any of your tactical team boys with any injuries?'

'Your radio was at the scene, George. It was used to summon police immediately following the shooting and *killing* of Sergeant Cutter. How do you explain that?'

'Well, I can't! My radio was in the locker, which is upstairs, *here*! It was kept here, and as far as I am concerned it is *still* here in my locker. I may still have the key but come on, you know that anyone here has access to that radio.'

Manto leaned forward. 'Didn't Sergeant Cutter lead the investigation against you eighteen months ago, when you were involved in another shooting?'

George shook his head. 'No. He was assigned initially I believe, but your lot stormed in and took it over. Cutter never uttered a word to me about it, and even if he had I wouldn't have had any sort of issue with him, if that's what you're getting at.'

Manto leaned back and pushed his thumbs behind his braces. 'I'm not getting at anything. It's just that you have a reason to be upset with Ian and with Langthorne officers in general. Maybe that's quite natural, maybe anyone would be in your situation.'

'I've just told you he had nothing to do with any investigation about me. I have no reason to dislike the man, quite the opposite, I'm sad that he's one of the victims.'

'Forensics have said that the shots were fired from almost point-blank range,' interjected Price.

George had to concentrate to hear him through the whooshing in his ears.

'He would have stood no chance and he would have seen it coming.'

George looked down at the picture. Cutter's eyes looked straight into the camera lens. Behind the fear there was something else in those eyes. It might have been sadness. 'Is that a question? I didn't shoot him. We were friends. I didn't shoot any of them, and if all you have is my radio at the scene then we might as well end this conversation right now. Then I can go and make my complaint about my unlawful arrest. Have you any idea how easy it is to slip those lockers open? Are CSI even looking at my locker? They should be. They should be looking for prints, or some link to whoever's touched it.'

Manto sniffed. 'Those lockers are in the hallway on the ground floor. Just about anyone in the station could walk past it at any time and leave a print on the door.'

George sat back. He turned towards Howard, who was beaming. 'I think that's the very point my client is making.'

Manto sniffed again and exchanged a quick look with the inspector. For the first time he seemed unsure of himself.

George was done playing their games now. He now knew this was a fishing trip at best and he wanted to be sure he gave them nothing more. He answered the remaining questions with "no comment."

* * *

George Elms was released from police custody shortly after the interview was concluded. Once the results were back from a urine test, he would return to answer to the drink-driving charge only for now. He had been given separate bail for the murder case, with strict conditions that would severely restrict his movements. Even so, George made the most of his release, enjoying waving to the custody sergeant as he left.

Howard Staples offered to walk him out. 'Well, that wasn't so bad, was it?'

'It could have been worse. I remember a guy I interviewed for a GBH. He spent almost two hours giving me the same story, and I was convinced he was lying. I had good evidence. I put a load of pressure on him, presented all the evidence and even got him to admit that his story was highly unlikely, but he stuck to it the whole way, never even breaking a sweat. We turned the tapes off and I said to him that he seemed to take the whole thing in his stride. I'll always remember his reply.'

'He said he was telling the truth, right?'

'Exactly! He said it's easy when you're telling the truth! I was thinking about that bloke today while I was sat in the cell. He had an absolute belief that the truth would be enough. You and I both know the truth is just a starting point for proving a lie.'

'Not always,' Howard said. 'But I have to say in this case they seemed determined to make something stick.'

'I don't think that will be the end of it either.'

'You might be right, George. You have my card if you need me for anything more. Any time.'

'Thanks.'

Before they parted, Howard stopped and half turned back towards the station. 'Do you miss it?'

From where he stood, George could take in the whole of Langthorne House. 'There's a lot of the shit I really don't miss, I think I'm better off out of it. But when I hear of a job like this, of coppers getting shot for no good reason, I do wish I was involved.' George smiled at his choice of words. 'And I don't mean involved like they seem to think I am! I used to be able to make a difference.'

'Make a difference, eh? That old cliché. The reason we all joined the job.'

George nodded. 'Yeah. Bit of an understatement to say that my career hasn't quite turned out the way I imagined.'

The two men shared a smile and shook hands.

CHAPTER 14

The media circus had begun. George turned on BBC News 24, and saw that his previous place of work was now under siege. A smartly dressed man stood in front of the Lennokshire Police station, speaking excitedly into an oversized microphone. A yellow band of text ran along the bottom of the screen, reading: "Four police officers believed shot dead in 24 hour period . . . Lennokshire Police press conference at 9 a.m."

Footage captured from a helicopter showed Langthorne House from high above. A large white forensic tent stood at the front of the building, surrounded by temporary fencing. In the next pictures, armed police officers stood manning the cordon that surrounded the station. A second aerial shot followed, of a different location and another white forensic tent, along the front of two terraced houses.

Eating a slice of toast, George shifted to the edge of his sofa. A cup of tea rested at his feet. His curtains were still drawn. A hangover lingered behind his eyes. He turned the sound up and watched the interviews with various members of the public, out on Langthorne High

Street. A young lad with a bad case of acne summed up the reason for the apparent lack of concern on the part of the general public. *'They're after coppers, ain't they?'* His eyes darted right and left, playing to the gathered crowd. *'I know that no one deserves that, yeah? But they do themselves no good the way they do what they do out on the street. Lot of people out here, they don't like the feds.'*

The camera returned to a makeshift studio, set up in a van parked against the cordon outside Langthorne House police station. While they waited for the press conference to begin, the newsman with the oversized microphone asked questions of a lecturer on criminology from a nearby university.

'Thank you for joining us. Is it fair to say that the police may have brought this upon themselves almost, by their own conduct when dealing with members of the public? Have they made themselves a target for this sort of violent reprisal?'

'Yeah,' George said out loud, 'and they deserve to be shot point-blank in the chest on their way home for it.' He shook his head, turned the television off and wiped crumbs from his lips.

The knock at the door made him scowl in confusion. He stayed where he was. He wasn't expecting anyone and his only visitors in the last few weeks had been either religious zealots or people trying to get him to change his power supplier. He decided on another piece of toast and got to his feet, his hearing totally lost for a second in a deep yawn and the whooshing in his ears. He stepped out of the living room and into the hallway. A second, more determined thud came from the door, followed by a scraping sound. This was not the knock of a salesman. George peered out through the peephole.

Nothing but darkness.

George cursed. The timer on the light outside his front door was useless. After some hesitation he pulled the door open, ready to shout at whoever was on the other side.

'Jack Leslie.' George said.

Jack's eyes were wide, his jaw protruding slightly. The knife held firmly in Jack's right hand was pointed directly at George.

Jack looked at him and appeared to hesitate for a second. Maybe it was seeing his former friend face to face. Maybe it was because George was a shadow of his former self, standing in front of him in a loosely tied dressing gown, barefoot and stick-thin. But it didn't last long, and his rage seemed to propel him forward. He lunged into the flat towards his target. George used the second's delay to step back and raise the hand still holding his plate. He swung it forward, and the plate connected with Jack's right cheek. The plate broke and George twisted away to avoid the thrusting blade. China crunched under Jack's feet as he drove the blade into George's side. George punched Jack in the head. Jack pulled back his arm in order to drive the blade again. George threw another punch, and another, all at Jack's head. Finally he dropped to one knee. George took his opportunity and reached over to grab the hand holding the knife. He pulled it towards him, trying to get Jack's arm up behind his back.

'Drop the knife!' George shouted. 'Drop the fucking knife!' He now had Jack's arm behind his back, but George could feel the strength returning to it. George pulled up as hard as he could. The blade was now inches from his face, pointing upwards. 'Drop the knife!' George managed again. Then Jack's hand opened and the knife fell to the floor. George kicked it away.

'What the fuck are you doing, Jack?' George demanded. 'What the *fuck*?'

Jack said nothing. His head dropped forward. George still had his arm in a lock behind his back, but he knew he couldn't hold him like that forever.

'Jesus, Jack. Fucking talk to me!' George spat the words at Jack's head.

Still no response.

George looked around. What could he do now? Jack was a big guy. George was struggling for breath, and with the adrenalin now seeping away he suddenly began to feel weak.

Jack was still on his knees and George spoke to the top of his head. 'I'm going to let you go, Jack, and we're going to have a conversation. And if you still want to stick me with a knife by the end of it, then so be it. I don't have the fucking energy to be fighting you anymore. You understand?' Jack stayed silent. 'We used to be mates, Jack, remember that? You know me.' George relaxed his hold and Jack's arm fell to his side. George saw the knife lying in the centre of the hallway a couple of metres away, and he took a step towards it. A sudden jab of pain reminded him of the injury he had sustained, and he touched the wound. His fingers came away spotted with blood. He went over to the knife and put his foot on it. He looked again at the small incision in his side, it was bleeding quite a bit, but probably looked worse than it was.

George turned the knife over in his hands. It was an evil-looking thing, a double-sided blade, one side thin and sharp, the other jagged. 'Jesus, Jack! What the hell are you doing, coming here with this?' Receiving no answer, he strode back to where Jack still knelt, head towards the floor. George stood over him, the knife held firmly. 'You wanna give me some sort of answer? You come here to kill me?' But Jack didn't move.

George snapped. He grabbed a chunk of Jack's hair and pulled his head sharply back. Now he could see Jack's face. George rested the point of the blade against the top of Jack's neck with the raised teeth against the underside of his chin.

'You came here to kill me, now tell me why I shouldn't fucking kill you?'

'Do it then,' Jack whispered. 'Like you did all the others.'

George pushed the knife against Jack's skin, the blade resting on the top of his Adam's apple. It would be so easy.

And then both their lives would be over.

George came to his senses and he pushed himself up off Jack's shoulder.

'I'm not a murderer, Jack. I didn't kill any of those people and I don't want to be hurting you.' George stepped back towards his kitchen. 'I'm gonna keep hold of this.' He dropped the knife into a drawer and stopped for a second to catch his breath.

'Tea or coffee?' George called out and waited, trying to hide his shaking hands, his body still tensed to react. He couldn't see Jack but he heard him shuffle to his feet. George reached for a small kitchen knife and put it in his dressing-gown pocket.

Jack appeared at the door, looking defeated. 'They're all convinced it's you. Everyone's saying it.'

'Everyone's been wrong before, Jack. You and I both know that. From what I hear this is all very personal. How much do you reckon they *wanted* it to be me? That would have been nice and convenient for them, wouldn't it?'

'No one's been shot since you got brought in.'

'Fuck, Jack. You know me. We started out together, worked together. You think I'm capable of what's gone on?'

'You avoiding the question?'

'What question?'

'No one's been shot, George. Since you got brought in.'

'Well, of course they haven't. You've seen the media coverage. If you're the man responsible and the media announce some other poor fucker's been nicked, of course you stop, otherwise if another job comes in the police know they don't have the right man. Think about it. This is proper serious. You don't get any more serious than killing coppers. Do you think they would be releasing me if they still thought I had anything to do with it? They had fuck all evidence on me, Jack. That's why I'm stood here.'

Jack looked confused. 'They still reckon it's a fucking copper though, one of us. It's gotta be someone who really hates police with a passion, enough for some real fucked-up violence.'

George looked at the kettle that had now boiled, a layer of steam hung under the window. 'And you think that describes me?'

'Well, doesn't it?'

George reached for two clean mugs. 'Jack, I don't have the will or the ability to be out there shooting police officers. Or grandmothers dressed as community support officers, for that matter. You know me better than that.'

'I thought I knew you. Before you shot your mate from CID. Even the chief constable ended up dead when he went out with you. That's never been sorted — at least no one told us. All we know is that you got suspended and that eighteen months later, you still are. So maybe you *are* capable of it, George.'

George found the milk and made tea. He slid a mug over towards Jack, lifted his own to his lips and blew on it. 'Maybe I am. And maybe you are too. You came here to kill me, so what does that make you?'

'I was first to Freddie when he got shot and was left to die. The first thing I knew was when that red button was pushed and we got the sound of a man fighting for his life. When I got there, I was just in time for him to *die* in my fucking arms. You ask what coming here makes me? The last thing Freddie heard was me making him a promise that I would find the bastard. That I would kill him, run a dirty blade through him and have *him* die. That makes me very different to the sort of man who takes the life of innocent people for nothing more than some sort of fucked up way to make a point.'

'I saw the pictures of Sergeant Lee — of Freddie. They showed me them in interview.' George's voice was soft as he recalled the images of the familiar faces in their blood-soaked uniforms. 'I knew him too. Not well, but well enough for the pictures to have an effect. I knew Ian Cutter far better. He was a good man, one of the old boys. He was good to me when I first started out on the detective route, and ever since. His picture hit me hard, Jack. You can believe that or not, I am long past caring. When I saw that picture, it was the first time since I got suspended that I wished I could come back. But I can't, and I reckon I never will. I am bitter, Jack. I have no time for the management at Lennokshire Police, and I would shed no tears if some of them were to meet their end thanks to this nutter. You should know from the people that were targeted that I had nothing to do with it. Nothing at all. Some young lad with a family, a wrinkled old PCSO, your skipper and an old friend. I'm not denying that I'm sometimes capable of violence, nor would I say that vengeance hasn't crossed my mind. I've spent long nights sat in this place with nothing to do but think. I've lost my job, all but lost my family and drunk more than I should, and you do get crazy fucking thoughts. All I'm saying is that if this was me, if I really was having my revenge, the targets would be different people.'

Jack reached for his mug, 'I shouldn't have come here. I didn't really think it through. I can't think straight at the moment.'

'That's what anger does when you let it fester in you. Feels like a long time ago I learnt that you've just got to let it go, or the only person you end up hurting is yourself.'

Jack looked at George's dressing gown. 'How's your side?'

'We both got lucky,' said George. 'I'll live.'

Jack took a swig from his mug. 'Seems I couldn't even do that right.'

* * *

After Jack left, George leaned against the door and exhaled. Jack had left his phone number scrawled on a piece of paper in case George "heard anything." George couldn't think why he should, or how, but at least it meant he could keep in touch. George pushed himself away from the door and paced back into his living room, undid his robe, and prodded the now congealed blood that marked his wound.

He switched the television back on. He had missed the press conference, but they were still repeating key parts. Helen Webb was centre stage, wearing what looked like a new suit. She was flanked by two senior officers that George didn't recognise. They were replaying the section that had sparked the most questions from the floor. Helen looked uncomfortable. She held out her hands to appeal for calm, and leaned towards the microphones roughly bunched together on the table in front of her.

'It is true that we made an arrest yesterday. That person was questioned extensively and has now been released on bail with strict conditions. You will appreciate that this is a live investigation so I can't release details, but I will say that it is also true that he is an employee of Lennokshire Police and is a thirty-eight-year-old male.'

'Ha!' George flicked the television off and made his way through to the shower. 'She can't even get my age right.'

CHAPTER 15

'Blimey, thanks, hon. What time is it?' Billy Toner said.

Sam Robins grinned as the figure in front of her sat up, the fresh cotton of the bedsheet falling away to reveal a muscled torso. He brought a knee up and rubbed at his face. Sam was wearing his white shirt, which had been thrown to the floor when they had arrived back at her flat in the early hours of the morning. He took the steaming cup from her and she sat, cross legged, at the bottom of the bed.

Sam chewed her bottom lip. 'Seven o'clock. Did you sleep ok?'

He grinned. 'When you finally let me.' They shared a smile and Sam slapped her knee. 'Right. I need to get moving. Do you want breakfast?'

Billy narrowed his eyes. 'No, don't worry. I'll let you get sorted and get to work. I've got stuff to do anyway.'

'Plans for your day off? Do I figure in your evening plans at all?' Sam teased.

'Well, today I've got a bit of football with the lads and then a beer after. Maybe we can hook up later in the week, eh?' Billy put his coffee cup on the bedside cabinet and stood up beside the bed. He stretched and walked towards the door. 'Mind if I use your shower?' He disappeared from the room before Sam could answer.

Of course he knew she didn't mind. They had been seeing each other for nearly six months now. *Seeing* each other. What an expression! Sam hated it but Billy used it at every opportunity. It was his way of making sure she knew where she stood, which was as far away as possible when it suited him. Sam sighed. She'd sworn that she would never get involved with another police officer, and especially not a firearms officer. Billy was typical of that particular breed. He spent all his free time in the gym or playing any number of sports with his mates. He wore his uniform just that little bit too tight and avoided all suggestion of any sort of commitment. For months, Sam had tried to ignore him, but his arrogant advances followed by periods of no contact, and his reputation as a bit of a playboy all kept her guessing. And those damned eyes. Sam knew she was being played, but she was drawn in nonetheless.

Sam had thrown herself backwards on the soft mattress and lay looking at the ceiling. Billy reappeared, rubbing at his short, dark hair with a towel. He scanned the room for the rest of his clothing.

He reached for a thin V-neck jumper and pulled it over his head. 'Stick that shirt through the wash for me and I'll grab it next time.' He gathered the rest of his clothes and fiddled with his watch.

'Next time? Next time, what? You fancy a fuck?' Sam was smiling but her eyes flashed.

Billy stopped fiddling with his watch. 'Come on, Sam, that's not what I meant. Next time I see you, is all.'

'And when will that be?'

Billy shrugged. 'I don't know. You know what I'm like. I've got a lot on.'

'Where do I fit in then, Billy?'

'Where I can,' he replied, his tone as cold as Sam's. Then he softened. 'I love it when we get together, you know that, but I don't get much time.' He turned to the door and picked up his shoes. He reappeared at the bedroom door hopping, with one shoe on. 'I'll give you a bell. We'll sort something out, yeah?'

Sam offered no reply.

'I'll send you a text.'

Sam followed him to the front door.

'Have a good shift, yeah,' he said and leaned in for a kiss.

Sam backed away. 'Billy?'

'What is it?'

She shook her head. 'Oh, don't worry.'

'You sure?' But he was on his way out. She caught a wink and a reassuring smile as the door clicked shut.

Inside, the flat was silent.

'I'm pregnant,' said Sam to the closed door.

CHAPTER 16

'Sarah?' George asked tentatively

'Hello, George.' She sounded hesitant, even via the phone line.

'What can I do for you?'

'I just wanted to call quick. Er, to see how you are. I had a visit — from the police,' Sarah said.

George screwed up his face as he took this in. Of course they had been to see his wife. 'Did you? I'm sorry about that.'

'Don't be.'

'Anyone we know?'

'Helen Webb.'

'I'm not surprised. She's going to be enjoying this.'

'She tried to give me the impression that she wants to help you — that you're not helping yourself.'

'Helen's one of the most experienced detectives I've come across. She knows how to work a source.'

'I don't want to be a *source*, George. Or a witness, or a victim or anything as far as the police are concerned. I thought all this was over when you moved out. They stopped bothering me for a while, but now here they are again. Telling me that you're murdering people.'

'I'm not murdering anyone, hon. Jesus.'

'I know. I told her that. I'm just tired of sticking up for you.'

George ran a hand through his hair. 'Don't then. Just tell them that you haven't seen me for weeks and that you won't talk to them anymore. They can't keep bothering you without good reason.'

There was a pause. 'I'm sorry it's been a while. I know you want to see Charley. It's just been a bit much recently.'

'It's my fault. I know I was the worse for wear last time you both saw me, but that won't ever happen again. It was a bad day and when you cancelled I had a couple of drinks to get me over it. I get so devastated. Then when you said I could meet you both after all, I knew I shouldn't, that I wasn't fit, but I didn't want to miss the opportunity.' George knew that he was rambling.

'Those are the kind of stupid decisions you make when you're pissed.' Then Sarah's voice softened. She said almost fondly, 'You've always been a stupid drunk.'

For the first time in over eighteen months, George and Sarah shared something approaching a laugh. George sat down. 'Is there any chance we can try again? Arrange a meet so I can spend just a bit of time with my little girl? I'll be on my best behaviour. It's been a rough time and it would mean so much to me.'

'Yeah, I think we can do that. Charley misses you like mad. But you have to be different, and by different I mean the same, the man that used to be her dad, when we all lived at home and had a normal life.'

'I know.'

'And that's the man I miss too,' Sarah added softly.

George didn't say anything. He'd learned not to rush things.

'I'll send you a text in the next couple of days. We'll have to work round Charley, she's got quite a social life now! I'll let you know.'

George was beaming. 'Thank you. I'm really looking forward to it.'

Sarah ended the call. George walked to the window and peered out onto the sun-baked high street. He'd spent countless hours looking down at this view and had always hated it. He imagined that all the people bustling around down there had not a care in the world. George stood alone above them in his tiny flat, a prisoner of circumstance, increasingly of alcohol, and of his own memories.

Today, though, he saw bright colours glowing in the hazy sunshine, shoppers and happy kids on their school holidays. Warm days at the seaside. George dared to think that the downward spiral of his life might just have come to an end. Just maybe he had turned a corner and, who knew, maybe he'd get his family back.

CHAPTER 17

Detective Samantha Robins was glad to be away from it all. Langthorne House was crazy. The media had set up permanent camp outside, and everyone entering or leaving the building was hassled by microphones and cameras.

Sam got into her car and nodded at the armed police officer standing at the barrier. As she waited for it to rise she cast a look over at the white forensic tent on the other side of the car park. Four reporters approached her window as she reached the road, soon followed by others. Sam spun her wheel and accelerated away.

Langthorne General was also busy, with a large police and media presence. The bodies of the four fallen officers were due to be brought here when CSI were finished with their in situ examinations. At least one of them was here already. The footage of a black private ambulance arriving was being replayed on all the national news channels. Sam had never liked the way the police uniform made her so conspicuous. Perhaps it had been more difficult for her than others — a blonde female in any uniform was an easy target — and today more than ever she was happy to be plain-clothed and inconspicuous. She checked her notes and followed along endless corridors until finally she came to a stop at a set of double doors that marked the entrance to Mansion Ward.

She slipped inside as a harassed-looking nurse rushed through on her way out. Sam went up to the workstation.

'I'm here to see Gerald Fedder,' Sam announced to the nurse on duty.

'Fedder?' The nurse did nothing to conceal her chewing gum. 'You family?'

'No, no,' said Sam, showing her badge. 'Police. I need to talk to him.'

'Bit late for that, isn't it?'

Sam dropped her badge back into her bag. 'Where will I find him?'

Clearly unimpressed by this show of authority, the nurse pointed in the general direction of the area behind her. 'You get one chance, one visit for half an hour tops. You want to come and see him again after that, you'll need to call ahead and ask the doctor for permission. You need to walk right through to the rooms. He's in number 4.'

Number 4 was the first room after the open ward which seemed to consist solely of elderly patients. Sam had no idea why her man had been put in a room on his own, but she was pretty certain it wasn't a good sign.

She had expected him to be alone. Two young children were sitting on one side of the bed and an older woman rose from the chair opposite. Their expressions were almost beseeching. Gerald lay breathing slowly, and Sam realised that she had not been very well informed about the seriousness of his injuries. 'Sorry . . . My name is DC Samantha Robins from Langthorne Police Station. I am investigating the assault on Gerald. How is he doing?'

The woman and two children looked at each other.

'Please, sit back down. I'll just ask a few questions and then we'll see where we can go from there.' Sam flipped open her notebook. 'Sorry,' she said again.

'Well, the nurses are wonderful. We've been very well looked after.'

'Good.' Sam smiled. She turned to the children. 'Hello.'

Two sets of eyes stared back. Both were around five or six she guessed, both very cute. The boy wore a checked shirt underneath his jumper. He seemed very shy. The girl had a bold, quizzical stare. She had on a pretty white dress with a matching hair band.

'Our grandchildren. Tommy and Carol-Ann.'

'And which one's which?' Sam asked playfully.

The girl rolled her eyes. 'I'm Carol-Ann, of course.' She kicked her legs against the chair.

'I see. Well, nice to meet you, Carol-Ann, Tommy.'

'Are you going to arrest the bad man that hurt my Granddad?' Carol-Ann swung her legs faster.

'That's what I'm here for, yes. I was hoping that Gerald might be able to tell me a little bit about who the man is. I didn't realise that he would be asleep.' Sam cursed the lack of information she had been given about this job. Langthorne House was a hive of activity, but all of it was directed at finding and stopping the cop killer. An assault on an elderly man didn't rate very high. Sam Robins was assigned to a job that would normally have two or three detectives at least, and the only reason she had been released was because no one wanted to use her on an investigation that might involve George Elms.

'Gerald was in a coma, Detective. He's not long been back with us, and he's still sleeping a lot. The doctor says that's quite normal.'

'You must be Gerald's wife?'

'Valerie Fedder.' The woman held out a cold, bony hand.

'Nice to meet you, Valerie. Like I said, I'm Detective Samantha Robins. I'm leading the investigation into what happened to your husband.' Sam reached inside her bag and produced her card. 'I need to talk to Gerald, get some details about what happened, you know, but I can see that now isn't going to be the best time.' Sam looked at the children, who had started to fidget and bicker.

Valerie glanced at her watch. 'Their mother will be back for them in about an hour. Maybe you could pop back later in the day after they've gone home?'

Sam looked at her own watch. It was just gone eleven. She could stop off at her mum's house for lunch and then come back. She could really use a chat with her mum.

'No problem. I don't really want to discuss this in front of the children anyway. When might be the best time? Is your husband going to be well enough to talk to me?'

'Gerald is quite compos mentis but he gets tired very quickly. Come back later this afternoon. That should give him enough time to get some rest, and the kids will be gone. We're keen to find out how the investigation is going.'

Sam nodded and said her goodbyes. She left the room, and walked back to the desk at the end of the ward, where there had been a change of personnel. 'Hi, I'm visiting Mr Fedder, in room four. Would I be able to pop back later and speak to him when he's a bit more awake? I really need to talk to him.'

'Are you family?' asked the male nurse.

'No, I'm with the police. We're investigating what happened to Mr Fedder.'

The man beamed. 'A police officer? Well, I feel a little cheated that you're not in uniform.'

'I prefer to be out of it,' she said.

'I'm sure you do. You can probably have a lot more fun when you're out of your uniform.' The man leaned forward. Sam turned away slightly and ran her fingers through her hair.

'So will it be okay to pop back to see him?'

'The doctors don't want him disturbed. He's not out of the woods yet, from what I hear.'

Sam bit her bottom lip. 'That's terrible. How long do you think he'll be in for?'

'A few weeks, easily.'

Sam played with her hair. 'A few weeks! My sergeant will be really upset if I don't get to speak to him soon. Sure I can't sneak back in a little later? It would mean a lot.'

'I'm sure I can sneak you in for a quick one.' The nurse winked.

As the door to the ward closed behind her, Sam already had her phone in her hand, scrolling through her contacts.

* * *

'Hello, Mum. I'm at Langthorne General. I'm just leaving, are you in for a cuppa?'

There was a hesitant, 'Er, we're heading out soonish.'

'I just wanted a quick chat is all, but if you're going out . . .'

'You're okay? What are you at the hospital for?'

'Oh, I'm fine. I'm here for work, Mum.'

'Well, okay then. What did you want to chat about?'

It was Sam's turn to pause. She knew her mum would be delighted. She'd talked about grandchildren more times than Sam cared to remember. Sam's dad was old school, he believed a wife should stay at home and raise the children. Sam wanted more. She had seen how empty her mother's life had been, especially after Sam had left home.

Sam knew that her pregnancy would give her mother's life some meaning again. The child would change her mother's life too. She felt heavy-hearted all of a sudden. Her hand went to her stomach.

She began to move towards the car. 'No, it's ok. There's someone else I need to see anyway. I'll see you another time, Mum.'

The relief in her mother's voice was all too clear. 'Soon though, eh?'

'Sure.'

Sam ended the call and got into her car. The interior was stifling. Sam drove away, heading towards the one friend she had always been able to talk to.

CHAPTER 18

'Sam!' George said.

'Surprise!' Sam hesitated, sensing that it might be a bad time. The hallway to his flat was dark after the bright sunlight outside. George had damp, uncombed hair and wore an open shirt over lounge shorts.

'Surprise indeed. Would you like to come in?'

'No,' Sam said. 'I quite like your dark hallway. If you could just grab me a chair.'

George smiled and stepped back from the doorway. He gestured for her to enter. He seemed a little hesitant, not quite meeting her eyes. He looked down. 'I'll er . . .'

'At least pop some trousers on.'

'I'll do that.'

Sam laughed. 'I would.'

George moved into the bedroom.

'I'll put your kettle on then, if you can't be bothered,' she called out.

'Thought you'd never ask!'

'Two teas it is.' Sam went into the kitchen.

'Coffee actually, I think.'

'Coffee? What happened to "tea for the English, coffee for fat Americans" then?'

George reappeared, tucking a creased white shirt into creased chinos.

'A few things have changed around here, Sam.'

'So I see.' Sam stared around the kitchen. 'You sacked the cleaner for a start.' Dirty cutlery was piled in and around the sink, and most of the surfaces she could see were stained. Cupboard doors hung open to reveal the mess inside. The remains of that morning's breakfast was attracting flies.

'My wife wouldn't appreciate you calling her that.' George gave a sort of laugh. 'What brings you here anyway? It's been a while.'

It had. After George's suspension, Sam had kept in touch, visiting or phoning once a week at first, but contact had gradually tailed off, and it had been several months since they had last spoken. George led her through to the living room, where he opened the ill-fitting curtains to reveal a room that was equally unkempt and cluttered. The daylight illuminated his sagging face, marked with scrapes and bruises. It was a stark contrast to the brilliant and mentally agile detective that Sam had once so admired. She could see that the mess of George's house was an accurate reflection of the state of his life in general.

'I guess I just wanted to see how you were doing. I thought maybe you could do with seeing a friendly face and a bit of support. Plus I have an hour to kill and need a cup of tea.'

George laughed. 'Well, whatever, you're welcome. I can't say there's been too many friendly faces of late — they've mostly been stern, judging, downright angry or whatever the hell you call the expression that Helen Webb wears.'

'Her expression has been a whole lot worse recently — well, you can imagine.'

Sam perched on the edge of a sofa, looking around at the mess. George abruptly turned to the windows and pushed them open as far as they would go. The sounds of the street and the passing traffic filled the room. He turned back to look at her.

'Something's bothering you?' she said.

'Yeah, I suppose so. I guess it's just my cynical detective mind.'

'Go on.'

'I haven't seen you in what, four or five months. Suddenly here you are, less than forty-eight hours after I become the primary suspect in a high profile case.'

Sam looked at George, standing silhouetted against the sun. 'You taught me a fair amount, Detective Sergeant Elms, some of which was worth remembering. One thing was *don't believe in coincidences*. I guess I should have expected you to question why I'm popping round now.'

'No offence.'

'I've heard all about it, of course I have, and PSD have spoken to me. They've talked to me about the possibility of speaking to you on the phone. They want me to somehow judge your mental state I presume, or maybe get a full confession. They want me to see if I can fill in the blanks about what you've been up to since you left Langthorne nick. They seem to have you down as someone who's become all bitter and twisted, whose life has fallen apart 'cause of what happened, and who is now doing the whole diabolical revenge thing. I ain't having it, not for a second. I know you're not capable of doing those things and I'm just pissed off that you're not at our side, hunting the bastard that's still out there.'

George seemed to relax. 'That's a relief, because the last workmate who visited turned up here swinging a blade at me.' George gave an unamused chuckle.

'Really? A knife? Who was that? What was it about?'

George shrugged. 'It doesn't matter. Seems even people that should know me better are believing what's being said. I think I managed to change his mind.'

'Well, one at a time then. Have you seen any of the news coverage?'

'Yeah. I've seen a press conference with Helen Webb and a few others. They're definitely rattled.'

'They don't have a clue, George.'

'That's obvious. You should have heard what they tried to pin on me. It relates to fuck all. It was an embarrassment.'

'From the talk round the nick it's just a matter of time before you're brought back in and charged. Seems a lot of people are happy you're the man.'

George leaned back against the window, a rare breeze stirring the net curtains around him. 'People are scared. They want to believe it's me.'

'People *are* scared, and I have to admit I'm happy to be out of uniform at the moment.'

'Ian wasn't wearing a uniform when he was hit, Sam. You look after yourself, you hear? You shouldn't be out on your own for a start.'

Sam laughed it off. 'I have to work on my own. They won't let me work the shootings because a mate of mine is the prime suspect. They're all out three or four strong and there's little old me picking up the rest of the work that comes in!'

'You can handle it, I'm sure. You still working Epping Hill?' Epping Hill, known as "Effingell," was an estate less than two miles from George's flat. It was the scourge of Langthorne, a nightmare for the management of Lennokshire Constabulary. It was full of drug addicts, drunks, criminals and gangs, with all the associated problems. Hence, a team of detectives had been put together to work solely in that area in an attempt to keep a lid on it. The idea had failed catastrophically. Sam had worked on the team responsible for investigating the jobs coming from the estate, the team that George led. She shook her head.

'No, there is no one dedicated to Epping Hill anymore. They still use me for bits and bobs down there but always just for advice. I've not been the lead investigator on anything Epping Hill since you've been gone.'

'And Paul?' Paul Bearn was another member of George's team, one that had been strong and close. Until George had shot him, his mind blurred with confusion, damn near fatally. But in a piss-soaked hallway, as George was led past in handcuffs, himself bleeding, terrified, and hurting, the medics had pulled his colleague back from the brink. Paul had been hit in the front of his shoulder with a rising bullet. According to the movies it's the best place to be hit, you will be cracking one liners and back to full fitness in time for the next day's action. But bullets don't follow the Hollywood rules. After entering the soft tissue of the body, they hit solid bone and then they break up, ricochet and cause havoc. In Paul Bearn's case the bullet had struck the underside of the ball joint in his left shoulder, shattering the joint instantly and destroying the nerves that cause the left arm to function. A fragment of bullet pierced Paul's lung, and medics at the scene had needed to decompress his chest before he stopped breathing altogether.

'Paul's back at work. He's on light duties but he still gets stuck in. Do you see him anymore?'

'I haven't seen him for a while. He still comes round from time to time but it's hard, you know? Paul's great. I've been beating myself up ever since it happened and I feel worse when I see him.'

Sam grinned. 'Is that where the bruising came from?'

George lifted his hand to his swollen eye. 'My arrest was a little enthusiastic, to say the least. There *were* ten of them! But how are you, though?'

Sam knew this was the moment to tell him. 'I've been better, George.' Her smile dropped away.

'Oh? You wanna talk about it?'

'No. You know me. I don't really do that.'

'I do know you. You want to tell me all about it and then never mention it again.'

Sam's face broke into a warm smile. 'Damn you! You do know me.'

'Well, in the last twenty-four hours I've been shot at, kicked, punched, dragged out of a broken window, arrested, and stabbed in the side. Just bear that in mind before you start on *your* problems!'

Sam's smile vanished. 'I'm pregnant.'

George's expression was hard to read. 'You'd rather be stabbed in the side, wouldn't you?'

'And dragged through a hundred car windows.'

'Not planned, then.'

'Nope.'

'I didn't realise you were settled down with a man. I suppose I haven't seen you . . .'

'I'm not. I mean, we're together but we're not, if you know what I mean. He's . . . we're . . . he's a twat, basically.'

'That's not a good start. So the dad's a twat?'

'Firearms twat.'

'Sam! Not a *pistol*!' George used the slang for armed officers. 'Let me guess. He's a gym bore, wears T-shirts a size too small and believes he's playing a part in *The Wire!*'

Sam smiled, despite wanting to cry. 'That's him.'

'You always said, *we* always said, never get involved with a copper and never, never go anywhere near a pistol!'

'I know, I know and I stuck to it . . .'

'You must have gone pretty close to him to get pregnant!'

'No, I mean I stuck to it to start with, but he wore me down. Oh, what can I say?'

'Well, I never thought I'd see the day when a pistol was able to wear our Sam down. I never thought anyone would, let alone a guy wearing his sister's T-shirt! What is he doing about it? Standing by you I hope?'

'I haven't told him yet. It never seems to be the right time.'

There was a silence. Then George chuckled, following with a full-on belly laugh.

Sam joined in. She couldn't understand how or why, but suddenly she felt like everything might just turn out all right.

* * *

Sam was walking down the street, blinking in the sudden sunlight, when her phone rang.

'How did it go?'

Sam frowned.

'The little meeting with our friend, George. How is he?'

Inspector Manto. Sam cursed silently.

'He's fine, considering.' Sam didn't hide her contempt.

'Talkative, is he?'

'Not about anything that would be of any interest to you.'

'So he said nothing that might assist with the safety of you or your fellow officers?'

'I think you might be watching the wrong man. Assuming that it's George you're watching.' Sam looked around the busy street as she made her way back towards her parked car with the phone to her ear. She knew it was highly unlikely she would be able to spot any of them. Any surveillance team worth their salt would be able to blend into this sort of environment with consummate ease.

'We're just trying to keep everyone safe,' came the smug answer.

Sam hung up the phone, feeling anything but.

CHAPTER 19

'DC Appleby, Force Intelligence Unit,' Bryan Appleby, known as Granny, said.

'Still on the same number then, Granny,' George replied.

There was a pause. 'George Elms! I heard you were dead, or dying!'

'Almost, mate.'

'And how can I help you?' Bryan Appleby had lowered his voice. George could almost see his old friend leaning into his phone and checking round the office in case anyone could hear him.

'What makes you think I want something? Can't I just phone an old mate for a chat?' Another strained pause. 'Bryan, I didn't shoot those people. I don't kill innocent people, just the guilty ones. With lasers from my eyes!' George tried a little chuckle.

'You laugh, Elms, but a lot of people are saying that you did.'

'You need me to tell you again?'

'No, no, of course I don't. If you hear something often enough, I guess you start to listen. My little girl's been banging on about how good One Direction are and I found myself turning them up on the radio the other day.'

'Well, now you know. I'm not going round killing cops, and . . . what's One Direction?'

They both laughed.

'So where the hell have you been? I was hearing that you were all in the clear, but you never turned up back at work. You milking it for the sick money, or what?'

'Kind of. If only it was that simple. I got cleared of any criminal allegations but the internal investigation goes on. Quick summary, they're never going to have me back, but while I'm still being paid I'll make it as difficult as possible for them to get rid of me. Plus, I've still got this damned ringing in my ears. Does my head in.'

'Well, I hope you're being a right pain in the arse. Would you want to come back?'

'No.' George was emphatic.

'So what do you need?'

It took a second for George to recall why he'd called. 'Ah, yes. All right I confess that I need your help. I need some information, and who better than the country's leading intelligence officer?'

'Flattery will usually get you everywhere.'

'Usually?'

'Usually. We've all had the talk, mate. According to them just answering the phone to you could put officers' lives in danger, maybe even our own.'

'I see. To be expected, I suppose.' George was in his living room. He went to the window, where he tugged at a greying net curtain and looked down at the street below. 'Well, let me just ask you a question and you can choose whether you answer it or not.'

'Go on.'

'Do you know Helen Webb's movements?' George let the question sink in, 'And would you be able to keep me informed of them?'

'Are you mental? Now you sound like a crazed cop killer! Why on earth would you need to know that?'

'Mate, Helen holds the key to me getting my life back together. I need to speak to her, but she's not exactly going to organise an official meeting or chat to me on the phone.'

'Perhaps you should stay away from her right now. At least while you're the prime suspect in a series of police officer shootings and she's deemed a primary target.'

'I need to speak to that woman.'

'Well, I'll tell you she *definitely* thinks you're a cop killer. What's your plan? Bump into her in the street? Or break into her home and kidnap her in the night?'

'I don't know yet.'

'She's scared of you. She's under constant armed guard. There's nothing more dangerous than someone who's scared for their life.'

'Well, maybe I can use that to my advantage. I might just get some truth out of her for once. Can you help, or not?'

'George, I am going to help you by not telling anyone about our conversation here, but that really is all I can do. They know that we're friends, that we used to work together closely and that I've shared information with you in the past that maybe I shouldn't have. They've taken all the local officers off the shootings for that very reason, so that no one who was close to you can help you, even if they want to.'

'Who's running the intel on the shootings?'

'I don't even know her, mate. She's North Lennokshire intel — literally from as far away as they could get.'

'North Lennokshire? Ryker?'

Bryan's pause was long enough for George to know he had guessed right.

'I don't know her, mate.'

George lifted his face to the sun streaming through the dirty glass of the window. 'Ok, mate. I appreciate that.'

'And my advice, mate, if you want it—'

'I don't.' George ended the call and regretted it as soon as he'd pressed the key. He'd put his friend in a difficult situation and Bryan had done the right thing.

Maybe Emily Ryker would think differently.

CHAPTER 20

'How are you feeling?' Sam looked down at the old man who sat propped against the white hospital pillows.

'I feel okay.' Gerald Fedder didn't sound okay. 'A little groggy. No need to make a fuss.'

'You've had quite a trauma, Mr Fedder. I think you can be forgiven for making a bit of a fuss.'

'I've been very well looked after.' The old man's hand touched the dressing that covered one side of his face. The surgical tape holding it in place pulled at his seventy-year-old skin, distorting the uncovered side.

'I'm Detective Constable Samantha Robins. I'm the one looking for the person that did this to you. Do you mind if I sit down?' Sam didn't want to be standing over him, she thought it might be intimidating.

'Of course.' He waved his hand at the seat beside the bed. 'I assume you're here to ask me a load of questions about what happened. I fear I may be something of a disappointment. I really don't remember much at all.'

Sam smiled again. 'Don't you worry about that, Mr Fedder—'

'Gerry, please.'

'Gerry. Don't you worry. Most people can help more than they realise.'

A nurse came in pulling a stainless steel trolley laden with jugs and a selection of biscuits. She spun neatly as the door shut behind her.

'Your tea, Gerry.'

He smiled. 'That time already? Always the highlight of my day. Not for the tea, you understand, but for the visit of nurse Helen here.' The man's one visible eye twinkled.

The nurse smiled at Sam. 'You need to be careful with this one. He'll be trying out all his best moves on you!'

Sam laughed. 'I appreciate the warning!'

'Did you want a cuppa, love?' The nurse held out a cup.

'Sure, that would be lovely.'

The nurse left both cups on a bedside cabinet, where pictures of Gerry's wife and grandchildren sat facing his bed.

Sam indicated the pictures. 'I met your wife and the two children.'

Gerald beamed. 'Smashing kids.'

'And your wife?'

Gerry chuckled. 'She'll do for now! We'll be married fifty years next year, you know. Imagine that! Fifty years. I can't remember what life was like without her. Wonderful woman. Are you married, Detective?'

'Sam, please. No, not just yet.'

'People don't seem to marry quite so young anymore. It was the done thing when I was a young man. If you liked someone, you married them. It worked out well for us but you need to take your time these days, make sure you've got the right one.'

'I can't disagree with that,' Sam said. Gerry looked into his tea. 'Gerry, the reason I'm here today is to talk to you about what happened, and to note down the important stuff. Then I can go and try to do something about it. I will ask someone to pop round and take a very detailed statement from you another day, but I didn't want to do that now. I want to be sure you're back on top form for that.' Gerry nodded. 'Are you willing to give a statement to us? One that effectively says that you support us in prosecuting whoever did this to you.'

'Well, yes, I mean of course I do. But like I said, I'm not sure just how much use I can be.'

'Well, let's find out, shall we? What do you remember about the day it happened?'

'I was at work. I don't remember too much more, really. I had the lawns to mow and some weeding to do, nothing that was going to take too long, but I was taking it real easy. It was hot, see? I remember that, it was so hot . . .' Gerry tailed off.

'Tell me what you do for work, Gerry.'

'Well, I'm a handyman really. That's what you would have called it in my day, or a groundsman, but I do bits in the church as well. Repairs and maintenance. They did give me some fandangled title but I can't remember what it is.'

'Do you work alone?'

'Oh yes. It's barely enough work for me, and I'm a doddery old fool. I get it done without any trouble, so there's no need for anyone else.'

'But there are other people about? I mean the vicar, and there are some volunteers I have details of, who work in the community hall.'

'Yes, there are. Weekdays it will generally just be me and the vicar, although Father Lawrence isn't always at the church. Sometimes there are people in the community hall setting up for the Cub scouts in the evening or for a weekend fête, but that's not often.'

'Was there anyone else with you, or that you saw on the day of the incident?'

'No. I don't remember speaking to a single soul that day. That isn't unusual. They pretty much leave me alone to get on with my work.'

'What's your relationship like with the other people who work there?'

'Fine. They're all good people.' Gerry paused. 'Are you suggesting that I could have been attacked by one of the staff?'

'No. But they could be a witness.'

'I suppose so, but the man that attacked me definitely doesn't work there. I have seen him before. He's been there a few times when I have. He tends to a grave there, spends a good hour or so at a time.'

'Which grave does he tend?'

Gerry lay back against the pillows. 'I knew you were going to ask that! I can tell you roughly, but I respect the people that are there. It's a private time, you know.'

'I understand that. Can you give me the rough area maybe? Something that narrows it down a little bit?'

'It's difficult, without being stood in the lawns. I could if I was there.'

Sam smiled. 'What sort of detective comes unprepared?' She reached into her bag and took out an A4 sized photograph of the scene. Taken by CSI, it showed the location where Gerry had been found, his position marked out by a white cone, with the gravestones visible in the background.

Gerry struggled upright, and pulled out his glasses from a drawer in the cabinet. It took some time to get them on over the padding. There were just over sixty gravestones, laid out in four rows parallel to the back fence. The grass in front of them was trodden flat. At one end a black steel gate led out onto an overgrown alleyway. The community centre and the gravel car park for the church were at the opposite end.

'It would be around here.' Gerry pointed with a shaky finger.

'So almost directly in front of where we found you lying?'

'If you say so.'

'Can you recall if you spoke with the man on that day? And where? I mean, did you speak to him while he was at the grave?'

'I just can't remember.' Gerry was visibly upset. He raised his hand again to his injured eye and touched the dressing. 'I'm sorry.'

'No need to apologise, Gerry. It's just that sometimes the right question can prompt some memory that really helps us out.'

'I don't remember if I spoke to him, but I'm sure the grave is close to where that cone is. I can tell you it will be easy to spot, it will be the best cared for — he always left fresh flowers.'

Sam could see that Gerry was distressed, and she didn't want to push him any further. It was time to leave. Further questions could wait until he was a little stronger.

* * *

The graveyard was quite a drive from the hospital. It surrounded the church at the centre of a small village called Eythorne. Sam parked in the church carpark. A welcome breeze stirred the trees standing in a row between the car park and the graveyard. Sam noted two other cars, a four-year-old Saab, a classic choice for a vicar, and a maroon Renault Clio that, according to the bright pink sticker, was "Powered by Fairy Dust." Tucked in a corner, almost invisible in the shade, was a black motorbike. Sam walked from her car over gravel that was worn, and in some places missing completely. She reached the grass, there was no sign of anyone.

* * *

Back at Langthorne General Hospital, Gerry's wife came back into his private room. She brought him a paper and his favourite wine gums. He told her again how sorry he was he couldn't remember much about what had happened to him.

'It's not your fault, Gerry. I don't think we should be worrying that you can't remember your attacker. We should count our lucky stars you're still with us. You might have suffered serious brain damage.' Her voice trembled a little.

Gerry reached out and took her hand in his. 'I'm not sure we'd be able to tell the difference if there was brain damage!' He leaned back into his pillows. 'I've seen him a few times before, you know, the man who did this. But do you think I can remember anything about what he looks like?'

'Don't be beating yourself up now, Gerry. Something may come back to you, but it won't if you try and force it.' His wife opened the newspaper and peered at the front page. There was a picture of a white forensic tent, viewed from above, and a ring of officers in high-visibility clothing standing round the perimeter of the car park where the tent had been erected. The headline read, "Four police officers slain in cold blood," and in slightly smaller letters, "Terror links probed."

'Such a terrible thing,' Valerie muttered and turned the page.

'I do remember something!' Gerry sat forward.

'What is it?' Valerie peered at him over the top of the newspaper.

'His bike! He always had his bike with him. Do you think that will help?'

'Who, the man that hurt you?'

'Yes. He would come on a big motorbike, one of them sporty racing things, a black one. That detective left her number, Val, let me give her a call.' Gerry pointed at Sam's card resting on the mobile table that acted as a dinner tray.

'Don't you worry, Gerry. I'll call her in a bit and let her know. It doesn't need to be this minute, and you need your rest.'

Gerry stayed sitting up. 'Pass me the card, Val, and I'll call her now. It might be nothing, but she said that anything I remembered might help, no matter how small. Maybe the bike will be just what they need to get this bastard.'

Just then, a nurse bustled in. 'Ah, Mr and Mrs Fedder.' She stood aside to let two men enter the room. 'This is Dr Ajhib and Dr Morrison. Dr Ajhib did your surgery, Mr Fedder, and Dr Morrison will be taking over your clinical care and recovery. They just wanted a quick word with you.'

'Of course.' Gerry smiled at the two men.

'It's an assessment. Mrs Fedder, I will have to ask you to leave the room I'm afraid, unless your husband insists?'

Gerry shook his head. 'No, it's okay. Val can grab me a tea, can't you dear?'

But his wife did not smile. She tossed the detective's card back onto the table. 'Well, I'd rather stay. I might have some questions myself.'

'Mrs Fedder, please feel free to ask us any questions you wish. But we will only take five minutes to assess your husband. You can come back with the tea and we'll speak to you then.'

Her husband waved at her. 'Shoo, woman!'

* * *

From the picture, Sam guessed she was in the right area. She was standing by a block of six graves. The front two both looked well kept: 'Janey Michelle Martin', read the first one, 'Loving wife and sister.' The sun made the white marble and gold lettering uncomfortably bright to look at. Sam opened her book and made notes.

A small step to the right stood a newish-looking grey stone, flecked with white. A square vase, also grey, stood in front of the headstone, with fresh white roses hiding the inscription. Sam leaned forward and tried to lift the vase but it was stuck in position, so she bent the stems and read, 'Anne Forley.'

'Forley,' Sam muttered aloud. 'That rings a bell.' She opened her book and took down the details. Beneath the dates were the words, 'Daughter, wife, mother, missed.'

'To the point,' said Sam, and took a step back. 'This is the one,' she muttered, scanning the rest of the graves. They were not as well tended, and Gerry had mentioned fresh flowers.

'Anne Forley,' she said again, and walked slowly back towards her car.

* * *

The man pushed aside a branch that obscured his view of the woman walking between the graves, heading almost directly towards him. Her eyes had been on the ground, studying the graves. He knew a police officer when he saw one. The moment he saw that *bitch* touch his flowers, he made for the path. If he ran, he could to get to the car park before the she did. His back was sticky with sweat beneath his bike leathers. He rounded the corner and his feet crunched on the gravel. Ahead of him he could see the woman standing by a small red car holding something in her hand. He slowed his pace to a walk, trying to appear as relaxed as possible. He could hear her now. She was on her police radio, relaying details of the registration number of the red car, a Renault Clio. She waited for a response and made some notes. He was close enough now to hear her clearly.

'Received that, Control. Could you stand by for just a minute?'

A voice from the radio blared, '*Standing by.*' Then she was walking over to him. He lifted the seat of his bike, reached in and put his hand on a black revolver. He held it concealed by the seat, and looked up at the blonde bitch who was smiling at him.

'Afternoon, sir. Nice bike.'

'Thanks.'

'Do you work here, or are you just visiting?' The woman produced a police badge and held it towards him. 'I'm DC Samantha Robins and I'm trying to piece together an incident that happened here a week or so ago.'

'Visit.' His right hand rested on the cool metal of the pistol.

'Often?'

'As often as I can.' He stared at her, trying to make her feel uncomfortable. Cop or not, she was still a dumb blonde. 'I come to the church sometimes, just to spend some time somewhere where I can be alone. It feels like I can get a pause in time here, nothing interrupts.'

She smiled. 'Fair enough. Do you mind if I take your details?' She flipped open a notebook and readied her pen.

'What do you need my details for? I haven't seen anything out of the ordinary. I can't help, I'm afraid.'

'Do you have a problem with giving me your details, sir? I'm trying to find people who visit here regularly so I can eliminate them from the enquiry. That makes sense, right?'

'I don't trust the police and I don't like giving my details unless I have to. I don't have to, do I?'

'Well, we could get into the parts of the road traffic act that make it an offence to refuse your details to a police officer when asked, when driving or in your case riding a motor vehicle, but I'm sure there's no need for that. You don't need to be getting arrested and your bike seized, now do you, sir?'

The man sized her up. His eyes ran up and down her body, lingering on her skirt and where her buttons parted above her breasts. Her phone erupted in her jacket pocket and broke the tension.

'Tell you what. You don't want to help us with our enquiries, then so be it. I've got a busy day today. Maybe I'll go and see if there's someone more helpful. You'll excuse me.' She turned and walked towards her car, talking on her phone.

The man followed her, careful to keep his footfalls as silent as possible on the gravel.

* * *

Gerald Fedder was starting to feel the effects of the day, but he had wanted to make the call to the nice detective before he gave in and lay down for a nap. His wife had left him alone for a few minutes while she used the toilet and possibly sourced a last cup of tea before her journey home. He found his glasses and dialled.

'Oh, hello there, Detective. Sorry to bother you so soon, but you did say to call you with anything I remembered, even if it was a small thing.'

'Mr Fedder, don't be silly, it's no problem at all. What did you want to tell me?'

'It's probably nothing, Detective, just a small thing, about the man who attacked me that day.'

'Like I said, anything can help. What is it?'

'I'm pretty sure this is true of the day he attacked me, but certainly I remember times when he has visited before . . . but I really don't know if it will be of interest to you.'

'Please go on. What did you remember?' Sam hid her frustration.

'Well, it's just that on the occasions when I've seen him, well, he's always been riding a bike, a motorbike, you know? Is that important?'

There was silence.

'Hello, Detective, are you still there?'

'A bike.'

'Yes, you know, a motorbike. A big one, a sporty sort, and black.'

'I understand. Thank you. I'm there right now as it happens. I'm going to have to go for now, but we'll speak later, okay?'

Gerald started to reply but the line was cut. He took the phone from his ear and frowned at it.

'I still don't think this is a good idea, having caffeine right now. You need to get some rest.' Valerie backed through the door, carrying two steaming cups of tea.

'I don't think the tea here has any caffeine in it anyway. It doesn't taste of anything.'

'Well, good!' Valerie looked at the detective's card which now lay in Gerry's lap. 'What did she say? The motorbike thing, is it relevant?'

Gerry shrugged. 'Who knows? I got the impression she wasn't too interested. Seemed like she was in a rush to get me off the phone. Who can blame her? She doesn't want to be bothering with a silly old fool like me.'

'Now she knows how I feel!' And they both laughed.

* * *

Sam stood frozen with the phone still held against her cheek and her hand on her car's door handle. She turned and looked back at the man standing behind her. He was wearing full bike leathers, and holding a large revolver in both hands. It was pointed directly at her.

Sam let go of the door and straightened to her full height.

'Hang it up.'

Sam ended the call and raised her hands, her phone still held in her right palm.

'Turn off the phone.'

'It is off.'

'Turn it fucking off! I don't want it being tracked.'

'Do you have any others?' The man jerked the weapon towards her bag.

'No.'

'Tip it out.'

Sam did as she was told, the contents of her bag tumbled onto the floor, including the phone she had been given by PSD. It had been turned off ever since.

'Kick it over here.' He gestured again, this time at the phone.

Again, Sam did as she was asked. The man inspected it quickly then slipped it in his pocket. He seemed satisfied and Sam knew he had good reason. No one was tracking her, no one even knew she was out of the office, and it could be quite some time before anyone noticed.

CHAPTER 21

'Emily Ryker! I knew I'd find you trying on jeans!' George said.

Ryker spun instantly on her heels and took a defensive stance. Then she seemed to soften when she saw the smiling face staring at her from his seated position. The female changing room of the Debenhams store in Langthorne town centre was the last place she would have expected to hear any male voice, let alone his. She had also dropped the pile of jeans she had been holding.

'George!'

'Surprise! And sorry, I suppose. I didn't mean to scare you quite that much,' George explained.

She stepped backwards. 'You meant to scare me a little bit then?'

'Not at all, Ryker. Besides, I didn't think anything scared you.' George wasn't joking. Emily Ryker was one of the most ferocious personalities he had come across in his time in the police. It didn't surprise him that she had earned herself an excellent reputation up in the north of the county.

She was small, but solidly built. Her standard wear for work was a hoodie and a pair of jeans. She also had a sardonic outlook on the world, and George had always enjoyed her company.

They had spent a lot of time together at one time. They had met while on training courses at police headquarters. George was learning to drive a flashing police vehicle and Ryker was already moving into the intelligence world. After their classes they would meet for a beer or two, mostly in the Wheatsheaf, a large pub near their accommodation block. Ryker had first visited the pub to watch her beloved Tottenham, while George just needed to get out of the formal surroundings of police premises. George and Ryker struck up an instant friendship. Both were young and single, and by the end of the week they were sharing a room. Ryker had arrived to sit her final exam in a wave of alcohol fumes. She achieved such an impressive result that she was immediately offered a permanent job in intel. George arrived at his final drive in a similar state and was promptly sent back to his room to get himself "sufficiently" sober. Five hours later, he too passed.

'Seems there's a fair bit to be scared of down here at the moment, your old lot are dropping like flies,' Ryker said, hanging up the jeans and crossing her arms.

'So I hear.' George was sitting inside the cubicle on a low bench under a full-length mirror. 'Officers certainly shouldn't be out on their own.'

'Like I give a fuck! Based on what I've heard, this fucker don't scare me in the slightest! Sounds like a right pussy.'

'Only you could label a quadruple murderer a *pussy*.'

'He is a pussy! The man's gunning down unarmed grannies, right? Give me a fully loaded pistol and I'll take out as many as come at me! Pussy.'

They were both laughing when they heard a woman's voice calling from outside the cubicle. 'Is everything okay?'

'Yes, thank you,' Ryker replied, looking at George and stifling a giggle. 'Just a bit of trouble getting these jeans on. Reckon I'll need a size or two up.'

'Would you like me to get the next size up in both styles for you?'

George shook his head. 'I need to talk to you,' he whispered.

Ryker called back through the door, 'No, no! I'll grab them myself if I need to. I'll be done in a minute.' The assistant moved away, and Ryker turned to George. 'Talk to me? Bit risky, isn't it?'

'I can hardly make things worse, can I?'

'Risky for me I meant, you dopey bastard. I get called down here to work on an investigation and straight away I have a little secret meeting with the only suspect, in the female changing rooms of Debenhams. I wouldn't mind but I only got here this morning. I haven't unpacked my fucking desk yet.'

Ryker chuckled and George knew he had been right to speak to her. Ryker could easily have raised the alarm and reported straight back to her superiors at Langthorne Police Station, but she was unfazed and just as cool as George remembered her.

'It's probably my old desk anyway,' George said.

'Hardly. That's a crime scene. Now what could you possibly want to see me about?'

George smiled. 'I wonder.'

'Out with it, then. Let's get the questions asked so I can tell you to fuck off.' Ryker's expression was serious.

'All right. I get nicked for this job, for all four jobs, and find they've got next to nothing on me. I want to know what else there is that's linking me to this.'

'Really? Don't you know? The radio at the scene was yours — is yours. You know yourself you just need reasonable suspicion to nick someone, and when you're talking about murder you don't even need that. Fuck me, we've both nicked people for less.'

'Agreed.'

'So what's your question?'

'There's more to it, Ryker. The way they went about my arrest, it could so easily have bitten them on the arse. They were trying to send me a message, like they knew it was me and it was just a matter of time. I thought they must have something fucking amazing. And if I was running that investigation and all I had was a radio at the scene, I would do things different. I'd get surveillance on the guy, give him a bit of rope.'

Ryker shook her head. 'Think about it, George. I mean, would you really? You've got officers dropping like flies, the media's all over it, the chief constable's all over it. Every fucker in a uniform is scared shitless to leave the nick and then you get this little gift, some actual evidence with a name attached to it. I know what you're saying. We've had weak evidence before for cash-in-transit jobs where we've let them run with a surveillance team on their arses, but if that fucked up, if it all went wrong and the bad guys gave us the slip, then worst case we would have lost another cash machine out of the wall of some village Co-op. If the surveillance team fucked up on you and you got away?' Ryker raised her eyebrows.

'Another copper might die.'

'They can't take that risk, mate. And if you were them, with that atmosphere and that pressure, you probably wouldn't either. And yeah, they sent you a message. There's a woman running this show, the Supernintendo—'

'Helen Webb,' George cut in.

'Yeah, exactly, Supernintendo Webb. I've only been in the office, what, six hours? And already I can tell you that she really doesn't like you, George. She had an opportunity to ease all that pressure, to give a positive report to the media and give you a black eye at the same time, and she took it, George. Just like I would have done.'

George shook his head. 'There's more to it.'

'I don't know what you want me to say to you, mate.'

'Why am I under surveillance? Why are they still paying me so much attention? I've counted fifteen different faces since my release, and there's a fixed OP on my front door overnight.'

'Belt and braces? I don't know about no surveillance George. I'm not exactly on the inside yet.' But her reply lacked conviction.

'You have to tell me what more there is! Why won't they leave me alone? Why are they so convinced it's me? They're wasting massive resources on me that should be out there looking for the fucker who did this.'

Ryker looked at her watch.

'Ryker, common sense must tell you that there's nothing to be lost by telling me. You know as well as me that all these resources are better off directed elsewhere.'

Ryker sighed. 'If I were to read between the lines I would say there's source intelligence.'

'Source info? Naming me?' George was incredulous. 'Who?' Source information was one of the most effective resources used by police. Information came direct from one criminal — the source — about another. Like all forces, Lennokshire Police spent a large amount of time, effort, and money nurturing sources at all levels of the criminal world. Someone in the criminal underworld had named George directly.

'Give us a break, George, I've been down here less than one working day! I don't know the full facts yet and I get the impression I might not get to know them at all. The whole reason I was told I was needed was for my experience in running sources. I was told that this was a sensitive job and I would be fully briefed when I got down here. So far I have been told nothing, I am largely guessing right now. I could well be wrong.'

George was agitated. Ryker was usually right. 'No, that would make sense. Source info,' he mused. 'A stitch-up.'

Ryker shrugged and pulled one of the pairs of jeans from its hanger. 'Who knows? But if you don't mind, I've already been in here too long.'

'Thanks, Ryker.' George got to his feet, noting that Ryker was suddenly avoiding eye contact. He decided to push his luck. 'So you have no idea who this source might be?'

'No, George.' She sounded angry now, and dismissive.

'This is my life I'm talking about, Ryker. Someone is trying to wreck it again. All I want is to know what the motive is, so I can finally get that lot off my back and ride off into the sunset with my family.'

Ryker stood with her hand on the door handle and her head bowed. 'Alright. I did some snooping . . . and it's *my* job and *my* life if you repeat any part of this conversation.'

'You know me, Ryker. You have my word,' he said to her back.

She stood facing the door. 'All I've got is a street name.'

George licked his lips. 'Go on.'

'He's local based — I'm guessing a big player in the drug scene. They call him "the Russian." That's all I know. I was going to try and find out who he might be this afternoon, but I'll probably have to wait to be told. It's all very hush-hush. Your mate Helen Webb is under a lot of pressure, George. From what I've gathered, she's running this source herself and she doesn't like the arrangement at all. That really is all I know.'

'Thank you, Ryker.'

She stepped out of the cubicle and was gone.

George remained standing in the cubicle for a couple of minutes, then slipped out unobserved and made his way onto the high street. The team of surveillance officers waiting outside had swapped around but he could pick out one for certain. George knew he could achieve little else now. He set off as slowly as he could manage.

CHAPTER 22

Helen Webb's white Range Rover Evoque bounced along an unpaved road. A front wheel made a popping noise as a large stone spun out from underneath it. She realised she'd passed the address she was looking for.

'Shit,' she said

Helen turned the vehicle round and stopped the car just short of a black iron gate in front of a large mock-Tudor house. 'Nice place,' she said sourly to herself. She knew that Lennokshire Police had found themselves meeting the monthly rent on behalf of the occupant. For now, anyway. Soon Helen would have her way and this piece of shit would be out on the street. She stumbled in her high heels up to the gate, and onto a more even block-paved path leading to an imposing front door. It was her first visit, and she stopped a few paces from the door to peer up at the frontage.

The door opened while she was still looking for the doorbell.

'I don't have one. That way I can choose not to be disturbed,' the man said.

Helen didn't smile. 'I need to speak to you, Mr Kavski.'

'It must be pretty damned important for you to make the trip in person.' He was supporting his considerable bulk against the doorframe, blocking access. 'And alone.'

Helen's jaw tightened. 'Not on your doorstep.'

Kavski stepped aside. 'Come on in.'

Helen walked past him into a large hall, which had open doors leading off both sides. In front of her was a wooden staircase. The Tudor colour scheme was matched by the large black and white tiles. It all looked expensive.

He led her through double doors to the rear of the house, a cavernous open plan living area, dominated by the kitchen, also in black and white. Light flooded in through doors opening to a glass-roofed conservatory. Beyond that was a swimming pool. A half-naked woman was lying on a deckchair in the conservatory. She briefly turned her head to look at Helen.

Kavski smirked at Helen. 'Tea?'

'No.'

'Coffee?'

'I don't want a drink, Mr Kavski. I don't intend being here long.'

'Then what do you want?'

'What I always want. You know the agreement.'

Kavski looked puzzled. 'Of course I do. Have I not been keeping up my side of the bargain?'

'You told me about the firearm. You said it was sold to George Elms by one of your associates. We arrested Elms based on your information. We searched everywhere and there was no gun. We had no choice but to release him.'

Kavski puffed out his cheeks. 'I told you what I had. I didn't realise I also needed to tell you that a man with his knowledge of police methods won't be keeping a weapon on his coffee table or in the glovebox of his car. It'll be somewhere non-attributable. That's common sense, surely?'

Helen knew he was right, but she wasn't going to tell Kavski that. 'Mr Kavski, I need to know that you aren't sending us on some wild goose chase just because you have history with this man.'

His tone hardened. 'I have no interest in wild goose chases.'

'You have an interest in George Elms,' Helen persisted.

'I did have. He's nothing to me now, and besides, there are easier ways to get rid of a fly in the ointment.'

Helen softened her stance. 'Alright. I had to ask, and I had to see your face when I did so.'

Kavski glanced at the naked woman, who appeared to be dozing. He leaned towards Helen and spoke quietly, 'We have an arrangement that is very much mutually beneficial. Thanks to you, I have worked myself a very nice position, and I'm not going to be rocking any boats, am I?'

Helen bit her tongue. 'Fine. Get back to your people and find out something that I can use. I need solid evidence on George, tangible proof that he's the killer.'

Kavski smiled. 'I imagine you do. You can't have him running round shooting cops, can you? Who knows who he'll be after next?'

Helen stared at him. 'I'll see myself out, Mr Kavski.'

* * *

Kavski watched the chief superintendent march back to her car, slam the door shut and gun the vehicle to life, spitting loose gravel as she pulled away. He checked over his shoulder to make sure he was still alone and padded up the stairs.

His call was answered immediately. 'Yes?'

'The police were just here,' Kavski said.

'And what did they want?'

'Nothing, really. They're just pissed they had to release Elms. They're scared and clutching at straws. The time is now. Where are you with Elms?'

'Where do you want me to be?'

Kavski raised his voice. 'I want you to get it done. I want you to stop playing games with him, that's what I want!'

There was a slight pause, then, 'I can get it done tonight.'

'Tonight?'

'Yes, tonight. It seems fortune has smiled on the brave.'

'What are you talking about?'

'An opportunity arose and I took it.'

Kavski settled the phone against his cheek. 'This is not a game. We need to be certain. You came to me because you wanted access to George Elms and the tools to make your point. You're where you wanted to be, now finish the job. And make it clean.'

'By the end of tonight, I will be finished. I appreciate what you've done for me, Mr Kavski, but don't pretend like I'm not removing a problem for you too. Tonight will be final and it will be clean, you have my assurance on that.'

'Just let me know when it's done.'

'You'll know.'

CHAPTER 23

George dropped to his knees to greet his daughter. He held her so tightly he could feel her heart beating. He brushed strands of her hair out of his mouth and his body shook with a single sob. He never wanted to let her go.

Charley squeezed him back just as hard, her thin arms wrapped around his neck. She had sprinted over to greet him, and was panting hard.

He heard a voice behind them. 'Are you okay, George?'

George opened his eyes and relaxed his grip slightly. 'I am, yeah. I am now.' His wife was watching him closely, probably to satisfy herself that her husband wasn't drunk. He wasn't. He couldn't have his daughter seeing him in a state like that again. He kissed Charley's forehead, inhaling her scent one last time. Then he moved back and they smiled into each other's eyes, grinning as if they were both six years old.

Sarah stood over them. 'She misses her dad.'

'Oh God, and do I miss her too.' George was finding it hard not to cry.

The seafront was busy. Langthorne's residents were determined to make the most of the prolonged summer.

The Elms family walked a short distance to where children were playing under the jets of a fountain, while the parents sat on wooden benches away from the spray. As he walked hand in hand with his daughter, George couldn't help looking over towards an ugly, concrete block of flats and bedsits known as Peto Court. The last time George had entered that building he had been armed with a stolen Glock 17 sidearm and was minutes away from shooting his best friend and colleague.

Sarah followed his gaze. 'Perhaps we shouldn't have come here.'

George shook his head. 'I can't avoid it forever. It's just a place.' Saying these words made him feel better. 'And besides, my girl fancies going to the fair.'

The fair was packed. It was situated on a large, stone platform, all that remained of the more permanent attractions that had once made up Langthorne's seafront in the days when a British seaside resort was still a popular holiday destination. Charley was already chatting excitedly as she saw the numerous teddies and dolls that were on show next to a row of plastic horses. Each chose a horse and shouted as the horses raced across the length of the display. Sarah's horse won, and she passed her prize — a Peppa Pig lookalike — to her daughter. Clutching her pig, Charley ran towards a stall where two boys were throwing hoops over glass bottles.

George and Sarah followed.

'You look well,' Sarah said.

'You lie well!'

Sarah smiled. 'Well, okay, you look like shit!'

'Bit harsh!' George chuckled.

'All right then. Er . . . You look well, considering.'

'That'll do.'

'You've really been through it these last few days.' Sarah's tone was kind.

'Well, it's not how I would have chosen to spend my time.' George didn't know what else to say.

They stood in front of the ring toss, watching Charley. 'They're never going to leave you alone, are they?' Sarah said.

'They will — eventually. Once that happens, I want nothing more to do with them. Then I'll be able to have a life of some sort.'

'And when will that be?'

'There's no case for me to answer. They just wanted to get someone in the door as quickly as possible, to stop any more attacks and to appease the media.'

Sarah scowled. 'You're the wrong man, so how does arresting you stop anything?'

'They were very quick to talk to the media about my arrest. That's got them off their backs. Now whoever is actually responsible sits on his hands for a few days, letting the police think they've got the right man. It's a tactic that can backfire — your standard serial killer is an arrogant fellow, so it can actually prompt another attack. I'm just glad none of it is my problem anymore.'

'So they don't actually think it's you?'

'To be fair, they probably did. But since my release, I would imagine their investigation has moved elsewhere and that will be the last I hear about it.'

'And what about long term? I know you won't quit.'

George turned to face his wife. 'I won't. Not because I ever want to work as part of that establishment again, but because I'd be silly to walk. They would love me to just chuck away my pension and disappear, but the fact is that I was injured on duty and I can't work. What happens if I do leave? I'm still at the consultancy stage with this tinnitus, no one really understands how bad it is in my case . . .' George tailed off.

'Do you still have the problems with balance?'

George nodded. 'The whole thing is getting worse. I end up on the deck with no idea what happened. There's no warning, no build up, I just go down. And there are some noises I just can't cope with, tiny little indistinct noises, an FM radio played low is enough to work me up into a real rage. I can't describe it. People think I'm mental. I've had to leave the barber's because I couldn't cope and I was close to smashing the radio to pieces. I lose all control, it's like a sort of confused anger and I just have to get away.' George was afraid it made him sound crazy.

It was a few moments before Sarah replied. 'I get like that,' George looked at her, not understanding, 'When that Nick Grimshaw comes on!'

They both laughed.

'At the moment they're paying for all the specialists to treat my ears, and the doctors keep telling me that I'll have to be pensioned off in the end. Lennokshire Police will have to take their advice but it has to be their decision. If they get rid of me, I get something out of them and they get rid of a right pain in the arse. Everyone's happy.'

'Well, not really.'

George thought for a second. She was right. He had lost his job, his home and the family he loved. 'The best of a bad situation, at least,' he offered.

'Are you pursuing them over your arrest? They beat you black and blue, George.'

'They're just terrified at the moment, Sarah. Someone out there is doing terrible things, and when they do get hold of the right person, I hope they give him a proper shoeing. It could have been worse. I had a solicitor in with me for the interview and I think he's making some sort of representation, but I have no desire to pursue it through the legal system. I'm done with that.'

Sarah stood a little closer to him to watch Charley take her turn with the hoops. 'How have you been though, George? Despite the last few days, you seem better.'

George took a moment to consider this. 'I do feel better. In a funny sort of way it's given me another kick up the arse. I've found that a few people I used to call mates have been very quick to condemn me. I could do with a clean break from it all. I think a move away from Langthorne would help.'

Sarah turned to look at him.

'Not too far though. I still need to be close enough to warn off all those boyfriends!' George nodded at the little girl failing to get her hoops over the bottles.

'We'd hate it if you moved too far away,' Sarah said.

George noted the "we." 'I couldn't do that. Despite what's happened, everything that I love is here.'

George and Sarah looked at each other and smiled. Charley was suddenly back. She grabbed her mum by the hand to lead her on to the next stall, and Sarah reached out and took hold of George's. Laughing, the family moved away.

CHAPTER 24

Sam had been watching the man's body language carefully during the call, and it had evidently rattled him. The call ended suddenly, cut, Sam guessed, from the other end. He stamped out of the room and into the kitchen. Sam could hear the sound of breaking crockery, followed by silence.

He had changed his clothes, and was now wearing a pair of dark blue jeans, a short-sleeved blue shirt and trainers. His pistol hung from his shoulder in a black holster. He was tall, dark and, yes, handsome, thought Sam. He had broad shoulders and carried himself well.

He stopped pacing and stood with his back to Sam. Through blinds pulled almost shut, his attention was suddenly on the movement of shadows past the window. The basement flat was sparsely furnished with a sofa, an elegant floor-standing lamp and nothing much else. The lounge was located at the front of the property and the window looked out onto a brick wall, marking the edge of the pavement above. From her position Sam could also see the silhouettes of people walking past, but nothing more. Anyone looking down would see a set of pine slats covering the window.

Sam had been dragged in the back way, where double doors led straight into a small kitchen-diner, and then through to a hall and the door to the single bedroom. The sash windows were shut and no doubt locked, with no sign of any keys. The bathroom was an extension crudely constructed off the back of the kitchen that took up much of the yard, leaving perhaps eight feet by ten feet of empty concrete.

Sam sat as she had been instructed, in the middle of the sofa, her back straight, her hands laid out flat either side of her.

He went back into the kitchen and came out holding a small stool, which he placed in front of Sam. He had made coffee in a disposable plastic cup, strong and black. He sat facing her, hands steepled in a thoughtful pose.

'Detective Constable Samantha Robins.'

'Yeah, you know my name. Now I know where you live, you might as well tell me yours.' The flat was on Dover Road, a street she knew well, situated in the northern half of Langthorne. It was a long road that snaked through some pretty poor areas, housing the overflow from the Epping Hill Estate, as well as migrants and refugees. As Dover Road moved towards the edge of town, the terraced houses and flats gave way to large detached houses. The flat where Sam now found herself captive was around halfway along. The fact that he hadn't concealed the location was a bad sign, and she was afraid. She tried to keep herself calm.

'You have no idea where I live. But I will tell you my name. It's Kane Mitchell. I changed my name to Mitchell at the beginning of the year — my family name is Forley. The name Forley should ring a bell with you, Miss Robins. Your police force is the reason I changed it.'

'No,' said Sam, honestly, though the name rang some vague bells.

'You'll certainly know my brother, William Forley.'

Sam took a second. 'I think I do,' she replied. 'Didn't he like to touch young girls, five or six-year-olds, if he could? Sure I know your family name, and I can't blame you for changing it.'

Forley's tone was hostile. 'He was accused—'

'Convicted. He was convicted of four counts and then he breached his conditions. He was a danger to children and a piece of shit.' She stared right back at him.

Forley jumped to his feet and began to pace around the room. '*Was*, yes, because you well know that Will took his own life in prison. He did that when he was sent back there for breaching the conditions imposed by the court, after he was sent to prison following an investigation by *Lennokshire Police.*'

'I was a good part of that. I interviewed your brother.'

Forley stared at her, evidently surprised. 'How did you feel when you heard that he'd taken his own life?'

Sam met his stare. 'I think I've answered that question.'

'Ah, yes, you referred to my brother as a *piece of shit.* Well, he never admitted the allegations. The so-called *victims* never officially came forward to the police. The whole thing was all pushed through by the parents, carers and school staff. Even the older girl who was a teenager never made any formal report. But your tenacious investigation convinced the judge and jury, and he was convicted.' He paused. 'How do you think paedophiles are treated in prison, Miss Robins?'

'The way they deserve to be, I imagine. And that girl wasn't a teenager when her ordeal began.'

'Isolation. That's what he suffered. Almost twenty-four hours a day. You'd think that the isolation would be the worst bit, but it wasn't. You see, he wrote letters to our mother *every single day*, so I know that the worst bit was the hour that he spent with the other inmates. Some of them had been convicted of the same crimes, and they would say disgusting things, treat him like he was one of them.

146

And right up to the last letter we ever received, he insisted that he was not one of them, that he was not what he'd been convicted of.'

Sam snorted. 'And you believed him? I get lied to for a living, you know, and your brother was not a very good liar.'

His voice was angry now. She had pushed him too far. 'Maybe you're right, maybe he was a piece of shit who deserved to die hanging from his own bedsheet, which he'd soiled in fear after threats from other inmates. Maybe he deserved the eighteen months of isolation, intimidation and constant terror that he suffered at the hands of HMP. You could make an argument for that. But my mother — my beautiful, innocent mother, who did nothing but love and care for us — she did not. She did not deserve those letters every day, to read of her son's constant torture, of his eternal, never-ending pain, when he swore he was innocent. She could do nothing. And she suffered.'

Sam shrugged. 'Okay, it isn't only the victims that suffer. But what would she have us do? Leave him alone until he gets to the point where he loses control and abducts, rapes and kills a young girl? I've seen it happen. Men who claim to be in control, to be innocent, can very suddenly escalate. They may not even mean to, they often don't plan to, but you're talking about a man who's turned on by children, who's getting more and more turned on and ultimately gives in to it.'

Forley stopped pacing. 'Still the assumption of guilt? You police officers, once you decide a person's guilty you can never be persuaded any different. History is littered with the wrongly accused.'

'And with people unnecessarily raped and murdered because a guilty person is allowed to go free,' Sam replied.

'My mother didn't deserve to be a victim.'

'I agree.'

'He came out and we had a chance. We had all clubbed together and sorted somewhere for them to move, my mum and Will, somewhere a long way from here. We were all changing our names to Mitchell and we'd have a new start. It got delayed. Your people wouldn't change his conditions quick enough so he could sign on in the north of the country, so we couldn't leave and we lost a couple of places. We had just got it sorted with probation, with housing, with everything. We were moving three days *after* George Elms harassed my brother, chasing him past a primary school and then falsifying evidence that showed him to be a danger to those children.'

Sam leaned forward. 'That isn't how it—'

'Don't you fucking dare!' Forley struck her backhanded across the face. She put her hands up.

'Put your fucking hands back flat!'

A small trickle of blood rolled down her cheek.

'Don't you fucking dare stick up for that man! He harassed, pushed and followed my brother. He manipulated the conditions to get him back in prison for the rest of his term. It destroyed us. Once Will was back in there, I knew he wouldn't last. He told me he wouldn't. The letters became desperate. He was writing more and more about how he wanted his mum to have a good life and that she couldn't have that while he was around. When he was out of prison he had seen the way his mum was treated by the people around her. George Elms had made sure that everyone in that shitty Epping Hill Estate knew what he was accused of. So they hounded my mum, saying that she'd bred a paedophile, that it was her fault and how could she live with herself! She would go out to get a loaf of bread, a pint of milk, some money, and she'd come back in floods of tears. In the end she just stayed in, ordered food online, quit her job, claimed off the state and wrote letters to her son. That was her life. Misery!'

Forley's eyes were glazed, looking beyond Sam.

'There was nothing left for my mum. She began listening to the people around her, and she blamed herself for how he had turned out and for not doing enough while he was in prison. For not keeping him alive. Even though there was nothing she could have done.'

Sam didn't react.

'She was a wonderful woman. When Will died, she died too. I mean, she didn't take her own life for another couple of weeks, but from the moment she found out, there was nothing left of her but a shell. She felt like she had failed everyone, including me.'

'So why shoot innocent police officers?' Sam spat. 'Blaming George, and going for him is one thing, but I know Jan Thomas. She was a nan, guilty of nothing worse than a bit of gossip. She had nothing to do with what happened to your brother. I bet she'd never heard of him. And a lad with a pregnant wife who was barely out of training school! Why? And what about the old man who mows the lawn and picks up a few leaves where you buried your mum? What was his crime?'

'Spoken like a true police officer. You sit there judging me, black or white, innocent or guilty. I want George Elms to suffer like we did, like my brother did. Like my mother. I've planned this in detail. I was just gonna gun the fucker down in the street when he walked out of his dingy little flat and be away before anyone knew what had happened. Easy. But then I thought about it. What does he get? No pain, no loss, just a bullet in the chest then darkness. Well, that isn't enough!'

Forley was pacing again, his face contorted, spitting out his words. 'Then I had an idea. I realised that I could put George Elms and his family through the same experience we had. Let him feel the exact same pain, the exact same desperation. In prison, a police officer might be even more hated than the paedos! They even put them together I hear.'

'So you shoot a few police officers, leave a tenuous link to George at the scene and imagine that's enough to get him convicted in court? Beyond reasonable doubt?

You're stupider than you look.' Sam's tone was calm and the strength had returned to her voice.

'He has history with the police, enough to give him a motive, and he knows the procedures. Of course, that on its own wouldn't be enough to get him where I want him to be. Although I'm pleased to hear they took out some of their frustration on him before he was taken to the cells.'

'How did you hear about that? I'm guessing from the same source that took George's radio out of the police station. You couldn't be doing this without the help of some dirty copper.'

'I can see why you're respected as a detective, *Miss* Robins. Yes. From the same source that told me who you are, and just how fortunate I am that our paths crossed!' Forley clapped his hands. 'Guess what? The people supplying firearms are also the very people that have links within the police. Seems some of your colleagues are very keen to get a little extra money, no matter what for. You lot pretend to be so righteous! Let me tell you, every one of you would be on the take if the money was right.'

'That isn't true. There probably isn't a copper alive that hasn't been offered a bung — I know I have. I turn it down for reasons that people like you couldn't possibly understand. Don't think we're all the same. So you found a piece of shit that was willing to take the money? Well for every copper who will, you'll find a hundred that will stick it right up your arse and drag you into custody.'

Forley smiled. 'I happen to think you're in the minority. I think there's no honour left anywhere in this world, certainly not in your precious organisation.'

'You're forgetting that you failed. You can kill me, you can kill George, but you won't get him into a prison cell. He's already been released without charge. Your only hope of avoiding prison yourself now is to disappear.'

'I will be disappearing, Miss Robins, you can be sure of that. But don't think I've finished with George Elms. I've got one last job planned, and George Elms will be pulling the trigger. He'll confess to it too. Then they'll have to put him away.'

Sam said nothing.

'I now have a hold over our mutual friend. He'll do anything I ask of him. Anything at all.'

Sam laughed. 'You think he'll do what you say just because you have *me*? Sure, we worked together, but we also worked with a million other people. He won't be putting his liberty at risk on my account.'

'You think you're my bargaining chip? Think again. What did I tell you about having a contact inside the police? This one has complete access to George's wife and child. He is heavily armed and he has their complete trust. He's willing to betray that trust on a word from me. George Elms just has to know that I can wipe out his family with extreme violence at any time. It's more than enough for me to get total control of his trigger finger. And I only need him to squeeze it once.'

'His wife and child? So I'm not here for leverage.' Sam's palms were suddenly clammy with sweat.

'Don't look so horrified all of a sudden! George will be known as one of the most notorious killers in history and you, Miss Robins, will be his final victim.'

CHAPTER 25

'What happens to the little girl now, Daddy? Now she's a mouse?' George's daughter gave a wide yawn, and rubbed at her face.

'Well, I tell you what, Charley, we'll see what happens to the little girl tomorrow night, shall we? When you're not so tired. Otherwise you'll fall asleep and miss what happens next!'

'Okay, Daddy.' Charley brought her small white teddy bear with one missing ear a little closer. Her eyes closed, and she gave a sigh.

George bent and kissed her forehead. He put Roald Dahl's *The Witches* down on her bedside cabinet. 'Nunnights, beautiful. How much do you love me?'

Charley smiled without opening her eyes. 'To the moon and back . . .'

'And round the garage twice?'

'And round the garage twice,' she giggled.

'Well, I love you more.' George padded out of the bedroom. He turned back to look at his daughter lying in the soft glow of her nightlight.

Sarah was in the kitchen pouring boiling water into a teapot. 'She go off okay?'

'She's shattered, bless her.'

'She settles better when you tuck her in.'

'I am available for hire — evenings, weekends and kids' parties!'

'I'll bear that in mind.' Sarah made the tea and poured out two cups, adding sugar to hers.

'I'll just have this, then I'll leave you to it,' George said, watching for her reaction.

Sarah didn't answer straight away. 'Okay,' adding quickly, 'But you'll have to come over soon. We can have another day like today.'

'Great.' George knew not to push his luck. They were getting on better than they had for a long time. He put this down to him finally accepting that he needed to move at her pace.

* * *

George walked away from Sarah's building feeling optimistic. It was a five-minute walk in early darkness beneath fast-approaching storm clouds. George made it to the silent bus stop just before the rain. His phone vibrated in his pocket.

'Hello?' George said.

'Finally, George Elms, it is time for us to talk.'

'Who is this?'

'Oh, you don't know me, George, but I've been building up to a chat with you for some time.'

'How did you get this number?'

'That doesn't matter.'

'I'm a busy man. Don't call me again.' George ended the call, but the phone rang again. He swore loudly and lifted it to his ear.

The man was already talking. 'You should try listening more, George. Just know that every time you hang up on me, I will kill another of your precious colleagues. I will shoot them all down in cold blood until you hear what I have to say. Their blood is already on your hands, George Elms. Now you will learn to do what I say or there will be many, many more deaths.'

George's tone was sarcastic. 'Well done. So you've seen the news, got hold of my number, and now you think you can call me up and make me do a silly little dance or something so you don't shoot another copper. Very clever. How about you listen to me. I don't care if you're showing off in front of your mates, you're winning a bet or you're just some sick fuck at home on his own. Don't call me again, understand?' And he ended the call.

* * *

Sam jumped almost clean off the sofa. Forley had just kicked the wall hard enough to loosen the plaster.

'Think I'm some fucking school kid, do you? Think this is a fucking joke? I'll show you a joke!' he said.

Forley grabbed Sam roughly by the hair and yanked her forward until she tumbled off the sofa. Still grasping her hair, he twisted her head until she was facing him, lying on her side. His other hand felt on the table for the pistol and he pushed the barrel into her cheek. He let go of her hair and her head hit the floor.

'Beg him for your life. Now! Beg George Elms for your fucking life!' Forley dialled again and thrust the phone at Sam's mouth.

She heard George answer, distant and tinny.

'Beg him for your fucking life!'

Forley kept the gun pushed hard into her cheek, but Sam said nothing. She clamped her mouth shut, tried to control her breathing.

Forley snapped the phone back to his own ear.

'Seems I will have to provide a different sort of demonstration. That's fine by me.'

George sounded less sure of himself now. 'What just happened? What are you talking about?'

'You hung up on me, you insulted me, you wouldn't listen.'

'What just happened?' George said again.

'What *will* happen tonight is a result of you refusing to listen to me. It is a message. You will receive a message every time you disrespect me, George Elms.'

'What happens tonight? What are you talking about?'

'You will offer me more respect tomorrow, I am sure of that.'

This time it was Forley who cut the call. He took a deep breath.

Sam had pushed herself up to a sitting position. She watched Forley through matted hair. The gun was now pointed at the floor but his finger was still on the trigger.

'Plan B,' he snarled. 'You're going to wish you begged for your life when you had the chance.'

Forley stepped towards Sam, swung his right foot and kicked her hard in the midriff, forcing the air out of her lungs. She gasped in pain.

She was crying now, the fight had left her and she could do no more.

CHAPTER 26

Helen Webb turned off Tenterden High Street towards her house and experienced a rare sense of relief. She had sent the briefest of messages to her husband earlier in the day, explaining that she would be staying at work for the foreseeable while they were going through a major crisis. She had received a one word acknowledgement.

They hadn't always been so distant. She had once been impressed by him. Richard Webb was a tall, strong, stoic man who took himself and his work seriously. Shortly after they met, Richard had left a prominent position at a well-established bank to become a partner in his own business venture, assisting affluent clients to minimise tax. It appeared that people would pay handsomely to avoid losing their money to the government.

Richard had driven himself and the business so hard that within a few years it was the first call of the rich and famous. His clients included any number of sports stars, actors, musicians and entrepreneurs, all exploiting loopholes in the tax system and saving huge amounts of money in the process. Eighteen months ago, his partner had relinquished his half of the business due to ill health, and Richard had bought him out.

Helen had her uses. Richard was able to show off his wife, one of the most senior police officers in the country, at networking functions. In turn, Helen could introduce her husband to senior figures in the police force at similar evenings, and bask in the kudos of being married to a successful man. And she felt the fact that he was black didn't hurt her image in the modern police force.

Their respective careers consumed their lives. Their twin girls were four and spent much of the time with their grandparents, returning home less and less frequently for weekends. The past eighteen months would have tested the strongest of relationships. Helen had needed to work long hours, answering some very tough questions following the death of a senior police officer and a serving chief constable. Richard had his own challenges. He had taken over a company that specialised in what people thought of as tax avoidance, just as high profile cases of celebrities doing exactly that were hitting the headlines and creating a huge public outcry. The government had reacted to this by closing many of the loopholes Richard was exploiting, and suddenly he was facing a situation where he was losing clients and unable to assist new ones.

Both had responded the only way they knew how, by spending longer and longer at work and therefore less and less time with each other.

Helen had not planned on going home, but she knew Richard would be there and right now, perhaps for the first time in her working life, she needed someone. Richard was a good listener. She might not even talk to him about the stresses of work. She felt like just lying with him on the sofa watching a film, being held for a little while.

Helen and Richard lived in a detached, four-bedroom farmhouse. Most of the land around it had now been sold off and developed. The barn that had once been a part of the same farm had been converted into three luxury homes by the previous owner.

The Range Rover came to a stop on the gravel drive. Helen could see lights on in the kitchen and bedroom. She opened the front door and pushed at the interior door that opened into a wide downstairs hallway. She picked up some letters and looked through to the kitchen. The night was still warm and she slipped her shoes off and padded along the wooden floor of the hallway, through the living room and into the large, open kitchen at the back of the house.

'Ah, Chinese!' she said, suddenly extremely hungry. She hadn't eaten anything since breakfast. The food was in its containers on the kitchen table, laid out as if it had just been unpacked and then left, the containers still hot.

'A lot of Chinese?' Confused, she counted five tubs. Suddenly she heard a thud, and a male voice laughing. She looked round the kitchen. It was as immaculate as ever but there were a few new items — a woman's handbag, not hers, discarded on a work surface; a bunch of keys with a Peugeot emblem lying on top of the bag; some women's shoes kicked off next to the back door; a woman's black suit jacket on the back of one of the tall-backed stools pushed up against the breakfast bar.

Another thud, then the sound of a woman giggling. Helen opened the first container, revealing compressed pork chow mein. She pulled a fork from the cutlery draw and dug in. She went on to the egg-fried rice, ripped open the bag of prawn crackers, and then leaned back against the ceramic butler's sink. And waited.

More noises from upstairs. The sound of bed springs, another giggle, then silence. Helen pushed herself away from the sink and, keeping hold of the chow mein and fork, walked back through to the hall where she paused, listening. She could hear a woman sigh. It sounded contented. Helen sighed too. She didn't have the energy to confront them. She felt even more drained than when she had left work. It could wait. She would tear him apart, but not tonight.

Helen swept down the hallway towards the front door, stopping at a board just short of the entrance hall where keys were left hanging on pegs. She slipped off the keys for her husband's BMW and continued out of the house, pulling the door shut quietly.

Outside, she pressed the key fob that opened up the BMW and lowered herself into the driver's seat. The car was one of the few things outside of work that Richard was passionate about. It was an M3, which seemed to impress a lot of people but meant nothing to her. She pressed the start button and the BMW purred into life. Helen threw the half-eaten Chinese food container onto the passenger seat. Some of its contents spilled out and the dirty fork smeared the leather seat. She set off down the drive, pausing to make sure the Range Rover was locked. Her spare set of keys were in a drawer at work.

As she stopped at the end of her drive she saw a small, new-looking white Peugeot parked at the kerbside a little way down the road. It was the only car out in a road where every house had generous driveways. Helen drew up just short of the white car and pulled the M3 to the left, until it made contact with the Peugeot, almost resting against the front wing. She turned the wheel further and the bodywork started to fold. The Peugeot rocked as the BMW grated slowly along its full length. Helen accelerated away, laughing for the first time in many months as the nearside wing mirror swung and clattered off the passenger door.

CHAPTER 27

George's phone shook and flashed in the darkness. Once again, he was lying awake listening to the rain. It was two a.m. and the screen read *Unknown Number*.

'Yes? Who is this?'

'This is your last chance, George. It could already be too late,' the voice said.

'Who is this? What do you want?'

'Are you ready to follow my instructions?'

'Listen, mate. Its two o'clock in the morning. I'm going to hang up and I'll be turning my phone off. I suggest you stop calling me.'

'George, give me just one more minute. Let me send you a picture message and then I'll call you straight back. If you've turned your phone off after that, I've clearly got you all wrong.'

George yawned loudly. 'Sure, whatever.' He swung his legs over the side of the bed. His ears whistled and buzzed as he stood and stretched. He scooped up his phone from the bed, and walked into the kitchen.

George made himself a cup of tea. He picked up the steaming mug, walked to the living room and peered out of the window onto the street below. Since he was a child he had always liked the rain. One of his earliest memories was lying in bed with rain lashing against the window, his mum sitting by his side. He had felt so safe then, so comfortable.

His phone beeped. He retrieved it from the kitchen and opened the message. He stared at the image and put his hand on the windowsill to steady himself. He studied it again and closed his eyes.

The phone rang.

'What have you done to her?'

'I wouldn't have done anything if you'd listened to me. I told you before, there is blood on your hands.'

'*My* hands!' George stood leaning against the window, his head bowed. Then rage surged through him. 'I will find you, I will find you.'

'There's no need to go looking, George. I have a car parked out of sight in the alleyway that leads to the rear of your flat. It's a blue Ford Focus. Make your way to it now. You'll find it unlocked with the keys in the driver's door pocket. There are directions in there to where you are going next.'

'Why the fuck would I do that?'

'You will do it, George. Because if you don't, you can be sure I will finish the job, and I'll make sure you get a photo that shows you exactly what you could have prevented.'

George thought through his options. There weren't many. He moved the phone away from his ear and kept the call connected as he scrolled back to the photo he'd been sent. As far as he could see, she was already dead. There was no job to finish. He put the phone to his ear. 'I want to speak to her. I need to know she's still alive.'

'That might be a little difficult, George. She is still with us, she's just not able to confirm that herself for now. She didn't take it too well, you see.'

'I'm not going anywhere without confirmation.'

George heard a scuffling on the other end of the line. Then there was breathing, harsh and laboured. He pushed the phone hard to his ear, his eyes closed tight and his lips pursed. He could hear the man's voice in the background.

'It's George Elms.'

'George . . ?' The voice was very weak but he was in no doubt. It was Sam Robins.

The man spoke again. 'I have some arrangements to make. You have ten minutes, including time for you to deal with the surveillance vehicle out front.'

George had forgotten about them. 'Deal with them? What am I supposed to do?'

'Oh, come on! You're the ex-detective sergeant. You have enough inside knowledge of how they work to be able to sort that out! And it's just one officer — seems they're losing interest in you, George. She's in the passenger seat of the silver Vauxhall parked across from the door to your flat. And, George, whatever you do, do it quickly. You have a tight deadline.'

The man hung up. George swore. His heart raced, and a cacophony of noise rang in his ears. His balance was affected and he needed to steady himself on the windowsill. Slowly he walked into his bedroom and got dressed.

On his way out, he slid open the drawer where Jack Leslie's knife still lay. It was all he had. He slipped it into his waistband and put on a rain jacket. He was starting to panic. He stopped at the front door and then doubled back to inspect the bathroom window, which gave out onto the rear courtyard. George wasn't sure it was possible to make his way safely down the twenty metre drop to the ground on a dry day, let alone in the middle of the night with a slick layer of water running down the tiles. He checked his watch again. He needed to get out undetected or he'd never make it. And nor would Sam.

* * *

The black motorbike and its rider vanished into the shadows as the light on the phone dimmed. He had used it to check the time. The ride from Dover Road to George's place was just a few minutes but he had taken his time to check that Sam was secure.

From where he had parked he could see the entrance to George Elms' flat, the Ford Focus that he had parked in the alleyway leading to the rear earlier in the evening, and part of the surveillance vehicle that was in a row of cars some thirty metres beyond on the opposite side of the road. The rain was heavy now, so heavy that he had to take off his helmet so he could see at all. He checked again. He should be out by now. What was holding him up?

He kicked the stand out and rocked the bike back onto it. He stepped off and looked across at the surveillance vehicle. He could get to it easily enough from here, using the cars and the shadows, and assuming that the occupant couldn't see clearly in the heavy rain. He checked that the street was empty.

CHAPTER 28

Despite the deluge of water over the cameras, Stephanie Larkin was glad of the rain. At least it gave her something to look at, at two fifteen in the morning. The water streamed down her windscreen, it was useless to try and see out of it, and Stephanie was grateful that she didn't have anywhere to go for at least a couple of hours. Her shift had been long and tedious. Six hours just sitting outside a bookie's, making sure no one left the flat above. The night sky lit up all of a sudden. The rumbles of thunder had been building for some time. Stephanie was not easily unsettled, especially by the weather, but the last rumble had made the silver Vauxhall Insignia rattle. She was sitting in the passenger seat, leaving the driver's seat empty as instructed by her covert surveillance trainer. According to him, anyone looking for persons in a vehicle will quickly check the driver's seat but will rarely look into the rest of the vehicle. The Insignia had been adapted for surveillance: an extra battery to allow the electrics to function for prolonged periods without the engine running, and a computer monitor fixed over where the FM radio would normally be, on which the occupants could view and record via three cameras fixed at different points outside the vehicle. The occupant could thereby observe while also ducking down into the interior of the car. Another welcome accessory was the Glock sidearm nestled in a holster in the passenger side footwell. Not that Stephanie expected to use it, she was pretty convinced that her target was well and truly tucked up for the night.

The rain continued to lash against the car. The noise was terrific. Stephanie prodded at the dimly lit camera screen in the centre console, which was operated using a touchscreen interface. She selected the camera that had been disguised as one of the forward pointing fog lights in the front bumper, and a grainy version of the road appeared on the screen. The place where she'd chosen to park the Insignia was near perfect, around fifty metres from her target's front door. Hers was the last car parked on the opposite side of the road before the pavement broke for a junction, meaning that nothing could park in front of her, nothing to get in the way of the forward pointing camera. She'd parked at a slight angle, not enough to make the Insignia stand out, but just enough for the camera to pick out the door in question. The science behind surveillance was simple — humans are in tune with their environment, the mind has expectations that things will be in place and only really focuses on individual parts of the surroundings when something moves out of place. In other words, don't move once you have established your surveillance position. Stephanie had stayed put and for the last couple of hours her view had been clear and unobstructed. Then the rain had started.

Her monitor display was red and green. The system could play back in full colour, but the display was designed to make things clearer in the dark. The visible objects mostly appeared green with just a couple of blobs of red where the streetlamps were positioned at points along both sides. The bookie's also offered a light source, which glowed red and bled over the target door when viewed on the screen.

Stephanie checked the cameras. The one pointing backwards was hidden in the driver's door mirror, covering one side of the car and anyone who approached the driver's door, and the third one was concealed in the high-level brake light that ran along the top in the centre of the rear window, which gave occupants a view of anyone who might be following them. Nothing moved. Stephanie switched back to the forward looking camera, leaned forward and squinted.

A figure was standing stock still in the middle of the road. The windscreen was still a river of surging water and Stephanie could see nothing through it. Her eyes went back to the screen. Had the figure moved closer? She'd already had one false alarm this evening — a motorbike with a wet-weather cover had looked like someone bent over. If you look at something long enough with tired eyes, you can make it look like whatever you want it to be.

The shape remained motionless. The small screen and absence of colour made it difficult to judge depth, but she was pretty sure it was standing in the middle of the road, and if that was the case it couldn't be anything other than a person. They were slim, standing with their hands either at their sides or behind their back with a hood up. They appeared to be facing in her direction, staring directly at the camera. Stephanie pressed the record button just as a sudden gust of wind hit the car and the rain slapped hard against the windows. A brilliant flash of lightning lit up the whole sky and the camera flared, the colours bleeding together. A couple of seconds the picture reappeared.

The figure had gone.

Stephanie peered at the screen looking for any sign of movement, while lowering herself down in her seat and feeling for the handle of the sidearm in the footwell. The figure had been in the middle of the road, so most likely it had moved onto the pavement on Stephanie's side of the road, where her view was obscured by parked cars.

'Shit.' Stephanie glanced at the radio fixed into the dash, and considered calling up. She knew this was not a good move — bringing a marked patrol car out would expose her cover. Still . . . what harm could it do if they just drove down the street? As long as they didn't stop for a chat and a piss-take, it wouldn't look out of place at all. As she reached out her hand, a noise at her door made her freeze.

A gloved hand rested on the door handle.

The car door swung open, and Stephanie could do nothing more than cower in her seat before the first blow struck her. The knife blade came down hard into her right shoulder, penetrating deep until it hit bone and skewed downwards at an untidy angle under the armpit. The attacker pulled it out, the jagged teeth of the blade ripping skin, muscle and sinew as it left her body, spilling blood. Stephanie had uttered no sound. She raised her left arm in defence, as the man thrust the knife in a second time. The cold, thin metal sliced through her arm. The man struck again, and again, and the ferocity of the blows pushed Stephanie's body down into the footwell, where the blood was soon deep enough to touch the bottom of the holster. The man took her loaded pistol.

He stepped back from the car, tossed the knife under the Vauxhall, and lifted his face to the driving rain. He wiped blood from his gloves and arms and walked away into the night.

CHAPTER 29

The Focus was parked in a small area of wasteland off to one side of the alleyway. Two large trees hid it so well that he almost walked past it. He pulled at the driver's door and it opened. He slipped into the driver's seat and checked around, but could see no further instructions. He looked at his phone — three minutes over the time he had been given. Maybe he was too late.

George had to calm himself, his hands were shaking and he grazed his wrist forcing his hand under the passenger seat searching for something that might help. Then he heard a phone ringing. A black Nokia, in a cubbyhole set into the driver's seat. George reached between his legs to retrieve it. The screen showed *Unknown Number*. George pressed the answer button and lifted it to his ear.

'You made it then.'

'Yes.' George wiped at the rainwater dripping from his hair.

'Do you still have your own phone on you?'

'Of course.'

'Throw it out of the window.'

George stalled. He certainly didn't want to be throwing that away. The car had manual winders and he opened the window on the driver's side, the rain suddenly loud in the cabin. He rolled it back up. 'Okay.'

'I said throw the fucking phone out of the window! Don't fuck me around!'

George peered out through the windows but it was hard to see through the rain. Whoever he was talking to had to be very close to be able to see his actions. He could be standing right next to him for all George knew. He wound the window down as a flash of lightning tore across the sky, lighting up the sodden alleyway. He picked a clump of grass that might serve as a hiding place until he was able to get back, and threw the phone towards it. He watched it bounce, but darkness had returned and he couldn't see where it finally fell.

'Listen to me, George. I have more contacts in Lennokshire Police than you could possibly imagine and I am also monitoring the police channels. If you call them I will find out, I will cut all communication with you and I will disappear. I won't come for you George, but understand this: I will take my revenge, and Sam Robins will be just the first. Do we understand each other?'

'What do you want me to do?'

'Do we understand each other, George? You don't want me to hang up this phone, it's all you have. Now, *do you understand?*'

'Yes,' George answered through gritted teeth.

'Good. Now drive to the Imperial Hotel in Hythe. Don't enter the complex, just pull up on the promenade when you have it in sight, and wait for my call.'

'What if the surveillance team see me leave and follow? I got out the back on foot, but there's only one way out in the car.'

'She's no longer a concern.'

George opened his mouth to reply but the call had been ended.

'Shit!' He brought his hand down hard on the steering wheel and lowered his head until he could feel the cold plastic against his forehead. He took a second then reached into the same cubby where he had found the phone. Sure enough, the ignition key was there too. The Focus was a little hesitant to start, it turned over eventually and he drove away. There was no movement from the Vauxhall as he passed it. He pulled out onto an empty road and switched on the lights and windscreen wipers.

* * *

The sea was calm, and peppered with raindrops. George opened his window so that the noise of the rain might calm his raging ears.

The Imperial Hotel was a large, square building. Bright white up-lighting shimmered off a white-washed façade, interrupted by grand windows. A Union Jack flag, fluttering in the breeze, marked the entrance.

George waited more than thirty minutes and was starting to wonder what was happening, when the Nokia rang again.

'Yes?'

'The Pennypot Industrial Estate. Do you know it, George?'

'Yes, I know it.'

'The main gate is open. When you enter the estate, I want you to drive through to the very last block where the road branches. Turn right and follow the light.' The call ended.

* * *

The Pennypot Industrial Estate was on the main A road that ran through Hythe towards Dymchurch and eventually on to Hastings. It was a small slab of land on the way out of town, and contained a custom car shop, a metal works, and a bespoke kitchen shop as well as more transient business interests and storage warehouses. The units were mostly arranged in blocks, all with a blue garage-style door against a grey metal backdrop with a single window in front. A couple had windows over two floors and were used as offices.

The gate was shut. George stepped out into the rain and, with a struggle, pushed it open. He followed the directions and came to a halt in front of a unit with a light shining in a top window. Almost immediately the Nokia came to life.

'Yes?'

'You are getting better at following instructions. Good.'

'What do you want me to do now?'

'Come in. The last door on the right and up the stairs.'

George got out of the car and went to the door. A large *To Let* sign was fixed to the corrugated metal above it. George slowly mounted the steps that were just inside. He came to a door on the first floor and stopped to listen. There was no sound and he pushed it open.

The door opened into what was laid out like a small call centre. The perimeter of the room still had desks out along the walls, but the middle of the floor had been cleared. The room was brightly lit and George narrowed his eyes. He could see a figure sitting on an office chair in the cleared space, and as his eyes became accustomed to the glare, he recognised Samantha Robins.

George stopped himself from sprinting over to her. Instead he tried to take in the surroundings. Sam herself was sitting with her hands behind her back where he assumed they would be bound. A black mesh bag covered her head with her blonde hair falling out over her shoulder. She raised her head. She must have heard him enter.

'Sam!' he called out. 'Are you alright?'

'She's fine,' the voice from the phone said.

George was taken aback. He had assumed that it would be someone he knew, but this man was a total stranger.

'How do I know she's fine?' George asked.

The man smiled. He was dressed in black bike leathers. He had short, dark hair and there was a red smudge where his crash helmet had pressed against his forehead. He was around thirty, slender but wiry. He walked over to Sam. George waited.

The man pulled up the mesh bag, exposing Sam's face. Her eyes were open, and wide with fear. She blinked in the sudden light. She grunted behind the black gaffer tape covering her mouth.

'Jesus — what have you done to her?' George took a couple of paces forward, but stopped when the man produced a handgun. He let it hang loose at his side.

'She's fine.' The man smiled and ran a hand down her cheek. Sam jerked her head away. 'She caused me some issues moving her here, sorry you had to wait. She's a bit of a fighter George, I can see why you like her so much. There might be none of that fight left when I'm done though, I'm afraid.'

George's heart sank. 'What do you mean? You said if I followed your instructions she wouldn't be hurt. I've told no one I'm here . . .'

The man let George's words die out. 'No, you didn't tell anyone, did you?' He pushed the barrel of the pistol against the side of Sam's head.

Her eyes widened and George stepped forward.

'Wait! *Don't!*' George stopped short, watching the barrel at Sam's temple. Her face was screwed up in fear.

The man took a police personal radio out of his pocket. He switched it on. He pushed the raised button at the top of the radio. The unit beeped twice and the screen flashed red. The man smiled and waited — ten seconds. Then a voice cut in, asking for DC Robins. The man threw the radio to the floor behind where Sam was sitting.

'My name is Kane Forley. You hounded my brother, William Forley, to death — by his own hand — in a prison cell a little under eighteen months ago. My mother took her life a short time after that. Because of you I have lost everything and everyone that I held dear. Now, police response time to this place is around fifteen minutes. The response will be armed.'

'William Forley?' George thought hard. He knew the name and now he started to recall the case. His ears whooshed and whistled and he started to feel unsteady on his feet, and nauseous.

'William Forley,' the man went on. 'He was systematically abused in prison. His last days were a living hell, while out on the streets of Langthorne, his mother suffered harassment. The police stood by and did nothing.'

'I didn't, I mean I don't know . . .'

'We had come through it and were getting on with our lives, but you got him put back into prison. You made sure he served the full sentence, his licence was revoked, and now I am giving you the exact same choices you gave him.'

Forley raised his phone to his ear, then put it on speaker.

George heard the phone ringing. The phone connected but there was no greeting, just a scraping, scuffling noise as if the phone was being stuffed into a pocket. George heard someone knocking on a door. It got louder. There was a pause and then a clicking sound.

'What is it?' *It was George's wife speaking.*

'Sorry, Mrs Elms, but we have to move you. We have information that you and your daughter are in imminent danger. Tonight.'

'Mummy?' *His daughter.*

'It's okay, honey. We're just gonna go and see Nanny. Can you get yourself some clothes out?'

'There isn't the time, ma'am. Can I suggest you get a dressing gown or a coat? It's raining quite hard. We'll get going straight away.'

'What threat? Surely you don't mean my husband? I've told you this is all ridiculous. He wouldn't hurt us — never.'

'We'll explain more when we can. We need to move now.'

There was a short pause.

She said, 'Okay,' and Forley cut the call.

'What do they have to do with anything?' George started to move forward.

'Nothing,' said Forley. 'As Detective Robins here pointed out earlier, there is often more than one victim. Take one more step and I shoot her. She's no more use to me now.'

George stopped. He was around ten feet away.

'Your options. The hell that my brother had to suffer, despised in a prison cell. Or die.' Forley looked at his watch. 'You have maybe ten minutes to decide.'

'What do you want from me?' George was struggling to understand.

'It's simple. By the end of tonight you will either be in prison for the murders of six police officers in cold blood. Or you will be dead.'

George shook his head, and then he looked up, puzzled. 'Six?'

'Six, George. You killed four in a twenty-four hour rampage that sparked this whole thing off, if you recall. Then you dealt with the officer at your home address. If they ask you about your change in MO, you'll have to explain that you chose a knife because a bullet would have been too loud. And it's more personal, isn't it? That bitch had been sat outside your house all fucking night, watching your every move like you were some sort of zoo attraction. You were angry, you lost your temper.'

'A knife?'

'A knife. Which you discarded under the car. That makes five victims. Concentrate, George.'

Forley smiled and threw the gun towards George. It came to rest at his feet. He nodded at Sam. 'Your last victim. The gun is from the surveillance car.'

George looked down at the ugly black weapon. There was blood on the handle. He could hear Sam sob behind her gag.

'You know better than any of us how it works. Your admission will go a long way, but the forensic links will finish the job. You just need to fire that weapon, George. I'm sure I don't need to tell you that my man is primed to follow my instructions if you fail to make up your mind. But whatever happens, Sam is a witness.' Forley walked over to George, picked up the gun and pushed it into his hand. 'Her life or your family's. That's going to be the easiest decision of the evening.'

The pistol hung limp in George's hand, pointed at the floor. Tears ran down his face.

Forley's phone beeped. 'The cavalry are coming, George. You have five minutes. The only way to protect your family is to pull that trigger. Make your choice.'

'I can't,' George breathed.

'You can be sure I won't have the same problem when I'm standing in front of your wife and child. I expected more of you, George. After all, you're the person who singlehandedly destroyed my family. Look at you. You're nothing.' Forley spat. 'I'll make sure they know, George, just before I do it. I'll make sure they know that you let them down, that you had the chance to stop it all and you did nothing.'

George pointed the gun at Forley.

Forley laughed. 'Shoot me and you shoot your family. You have no idea who is waiting to pull the trigger in my place. They have very strict instructions too, George. I'm sure you can work out what happens if they don't hear from me. Seems the police are pretty easy to buy since the government decided that you lot are worth fuck-all.'

'Who would?' George lowered the gun slightly.

'Oh, and Ed Kavski said to say hi.'

'Kavski?' George's eyes widened.

'Seems he's got a bit of a history with you, George. When he found out what I wanted to do, he couldn't wait to help.'

George didn't reply.

Forley looked at his watch. 'You have two minutes.'

Forley backed away slightly, watching. George held the pistol pointed at the floor, but his finger remained on the trigger. He turned back to Sam. Her eyes were full of tears and she was slowly shaking her head as George looked at her.

Forley clapped his hands, and George and Sam flinched. 'Let's make this interesting.' He went over to Sam, bent down and ripped the black tape from her mouth. He backed away, pulling his mobile phone from his pocket. 'You have ten seconds, George, or I make the call and your wife and child are dead.'

George's head was whooshing so loudly that it almost blocked out all other sounds, but he heard Sam speak.

'You have to call it in, George.' Her voice was quite calm, as though she was trying to reason with him. 'He's lying, George. He's playing a game. No one's going to do that, no copper on earth.'

George lowered his eyes. 'I can't . . . take the risk.'

'George, please think this through. You're an innocent man and you'll get your life back, but if you shoot that gun, you'll lose everything and that piece of shit walks free.'

George moved forward like an automaton. He bent down and picked up the tape, lying on the floor beside Sam's chair.

Sam's voice rose. 'What are you doing, George? George!' He tried to be gentle as he pushed the tape back over her mouth but she bucked in the seat and the tape fell loose. He was rougher now as he tucked the gun in his trousers and pushed the tape back across her mouth.

George held the weapon steady in both hands, and Sam closed her eyes and fell still. 'I'm so sorry. There's no other way for them.'

George stepped forward. One arm came away from the gun and he wrapped it round Sam. His cheek rested against hers for a moment. His right hand pushed the barrel of the weapon hard into the fleshy area where chest met armpit. As he pulled the trigger he hooked the underside of the chair with his foot and pulled down with his left hand, rocking the chair hard backwards and letting it go. Blood leaked from Sam's armpit and the back of her head hit the floor, knocking her out. Sam appeared to be dead.

But Forley wasn't fooled. He had produced another pistol, and now he pointed it at Sam, lying still and silent on the floor. He stood over her. George was frozen to the spot, gun loose in his right hand. He watched as Forley licked his lips and steadied himself, and then pulled the trigger three times.

George didn't see Forley leave. He threw the gun to the ground as if it was red hot and his head bent forward. He was weeping, and the noise in his ears roared so loudly that he didn't hear the sirens. Then he saw flashes of blue against the slit windows.

Clumsily he stumbled to his feet. He looked at Sam, at the blood pooling around her, and knew that she was gone.

George now heard the sirens. They were closer, the noise cutting through the tinnitus. He picked up the gun and stuffed it in his pocket. He stumbled towards the door that Forley had left through minutes before. A green emergency exit sign was illuminated above his head with an arrow pointing left and he ran in the direction it pointed. At the end of this corridor he opened a door marked "Fire Exit," and was out of the building, running down metal steps with soaking handrails. George turned sharp right and ran along the line of a fence at the back of the estate. He had no idea where he was going.

Tears still stung his eyes and he ran blindly into the night.

CHAPTER 30

George tugged his jacket off and threw it high, holding one of the sleeves so it fell over the top of the perimeter fence. The fence was solid, slick with water and topped with coiled razor wire. He backed away ten paces or so and then ran at it, throwing himself as high as he could. His hands and feet desperately felt for grip. He struggled to the top and gingerly picked his way over the razor wire. His weight pushed his coat into the barbs and he had to abandon it as he dropped to the other side. He suffered a couple of nicks on his hands and arms. George barely noticed.

He dropped onto a well-worn footpath that ran along the canal bank and away from the industrial estate. It was a short sprint before houses started appearing, their back gardens easily accessible from the path. George climbed a low fence to cut through. He jogged up a long garden between two houses, coming out in the middle of what looked like a cul-de-sac. The house opposite had a sporty-looking Audi in the drive. George ran across the road. The house was in darkness. The rear had double doors leading through to the kitchen. He could see the key sticking out the other side of the door. The garden contained a rockery around a small pond and George picked up one of the larger rocks. It took two attempts to gain entry through the double-glazed door and it was very noisy.

George made his way quickly through the house, his eyes darting around surfaces and walls, looking for the Audi keys. A light suddenly flicked on from upstairs, it illuminated the keys lying on top of a cabinet in the hall.

'What are you doing!' someone shouted from the top of the stairs.

George looked up to where a stocky man in boxer shorts was coming down. George scooped up the keys.

'Oi!' he shouted again.

George pulled the pistol from his waistband and pointed it directly up the stairs. 'Don't be stupid,' he growled.

A little girl appeared. She was rubbing sleep from her eyes, her hair a mess, clutching a brown bear.

'What's the matter, Daddy?'

The man quickly pulled her behind his body. He grabbed her too hard and she yelped in pain and started to cry.

'What's going on?' said a female voice. A woman came onto the landing. She looked down at George, and at the gun pointing up at them.

'Don't be stupid,' George said again. He hesitated for just a second and fixed on the young girl who must have been a similar age to Charley. 'I'm sorry,' he muttered, and then he was gone.

CHAPTER 31

Sevenscore police complex just outside Canterbury had once been the proud hub of roads policing for the whole county. Vehicle repair and servicing had all been moved to the site, and a large warehouse structure had been added to the existing office block for this purpose.

Police activity at the site had all but disappeared in the last few years, with government cuts forcing a change in the policing structure and the deployment of resources. Sevenscore was still the service and repair shop for the east of the county, but its yard of crash-damaged, old and just plain exhausted police vehicles was an apt reflection of the state of the force as a whole.

The whole of the top floor had sat empty and silent for more than a year. The only movement had come from the men's urinal which still obediently flushed itself thanks to a long forgotten timer. There, at 3 a.m., Detective Inspector Price dried his hands with a coarse paper towel. He leaned forward and peered at his reflection in a rust-spotted mirror. He sighed. He looked like shit, which made sense, he also felt like shit. He had been instructed to get some sleep and had tried. A room on the ground floor had sofas in front of an old tube television, as well as metal shutters covering every window, that kept the air thick and muggy. He had lasted just thirty minutes in the heat, and then, amid the heavy breathing, snoring and general fidgeting of the others around him, had made his escape. Not for the first time he wished he had asked to go home. He had been close, getting as far as broaching the subject with the chief superintendent.

'Don't you think we'd all benefit from a good rest? I mean we've had a few long days, maybe we're not at our best.'

She had agreed. 'Maybe you're right. Get everyone rested. I think there's a rest room on the ground floor with some sofas you can use.'

Helen herself had left for home shortly afterwards. She had said that she was going home to freshen up and that she needed to see her husband, but Price got the impression that she might not be coming back. To his surprise she had returned after just an hour, and seemed in no mood to speak when she bustled back in.

They'd been moved to Sevenscore for security reasons. There was no public access, and the high gates and fences certainly provided peace of mind. Furthermore, no police officers had any business at the site unless invited, or more accurately summoned, by Helen Webb. Sevenscore also had a ready-made incident room, furnished with systems, phones, area maps, and all the equipment necessary for dealing with a major incident. A bearded detective sergeant, who was a Tolkien fan, had referred to it as Lennokshire Police's *Helm's Deep*.

The incident room was quiet. It was the middle of the night and two bored detectives were watching calls come in on the screen, occasionally clicking to see live updates as the main control room typed them on.

The sudden activation of an emergency button made everyone snap to attention. The two detectives turned their attention to the screen that identified the source. It was a radio belonging to Detective Constable Samantha Robins. They grabbed a radio that was charging in a cradle on the desk and turned it up, just as Sam's radio gave ten seconds of silence.

'Nothing?' The two exchanged a glance. They were frozen to the spot for a couple more seconds as they listened to the control room calling DC Robins, trying to conceal the panic in their voices.

'We'd better get the boss.'

* * *

Helen Webb and Inspector Price made it to the incident room at the same time. Helen was bleary-eyed, having actually been asleep on a soft chair in a room she was using as an office, when a breathless detective burst into her room, struggling to form the right words. The superintendent brushed past her and made her way straight to the incident room. Inspector Price had heard her running and had followed. Both stared at the screens still flashing red. Distorted radio traffic sounded loud through the room's speakers.

Someone called over to the superintendent. 'We have another activation. It's Samantha Robins, she's a detective out of Langthorne House.'

Helen nodded. She knew Sam well enough. 'Where?'

'An industrial estate in Hythe. The radio signal isn't great down there so we've got a group of four possible units.'

For a second Helen's cold professional demeanour dropped away. 'Fuck! What is she doing there?'

'She shouldn't be on duty, ma'am. She was early turn yesterday and today but it doesn't look like she booked off.'

'She didn't book off? Why are we only just finding out about this now?' Helen paced over to a computer. 'Fuck,' Helen said again as she stumbled over typing her password. Detectives were something of a law unto themselves. It wasn't unusual for them to work all day and fail to log on, forgetting to log out their call sign as they left. Helen had sent out a message just a day ago reminding everyone of the importance of booking on and off the system in order to stay safe. Even if this was now being adhered to, it was clear that the people tasked with monitoring it had failed.

'Ma'am, the first patrols are arriving now.'

'Firearms?'

'Yes, yes – Foxtrot One.'

The room waited. Helen Webb went on air. She announced that she was taking command of the incident and immediately called for all patrols to maintain radio silence, with the exception of the Foxtrot patrol, until it was clear what was going on. The tension in the room mounted. People kept filing in, all silent, looking at each other.

'Foxtrot one.' The voice spoke too close to the microphone and it came across distorted, panicked. *'We need a medic here. On the hurry up.'*

CHAPTER 32

The world was nothing but a sodden blur through the darkened windows of the Audi. It was an S3 model and the turbo-charged engine screamed with delight as George worked it hard, keeping the car on the road through the bends, and powering into the straights. On any other day George would have enjoyed this. In his youth he had owned and loved a lively hot hatch until the inevitable had happened and he finished upside down in a ditch with the wheels spinning.

Tonight, George's tinnitus whooshed, and he could hear every panicked beat of his heart amid the constant racket in his ears. His hands gripped the steering wheel, palms clammy, knuckles white. His eyes were wide, his throat dry and tight. His brain teemed with what he had seen, what he could have done, what he should do now. He had no plan save to drive to where he believed his wife and child were in extreme danger, and *somehow* take them away to safety. He had no idea how he was going to do this, no idea what "safe" even was anymore. George kept glancing at the passenger seat where the black pistol slid and bumped around like an excited child demanding that they go faster.

George pulled out onto the main A Road that would take him back towards Langthorne, from where he intended to head for the more rural roads in order to bypass the town. He knew from the phone call that his wife and child were headed to his mother-in-law who lived on the outskirts of Hastingleigh, a tiny village made up of well-spaced large houses. Sarah's mother's house was the only one at the end of a twisty road flanked by wood and field. There was only one way in and out.

* * *

The police medics had tried to revive their fallen colleague. When the wounds had stopped leaking, and there was no pulse and no breathing, the three medics had stretchered Sam to a waiting ambulance.

Then the incident room, still reeling from news of Sam's death, received a reply from a forgotten request to check in on the surveillance officer tasked with observing George Elms. It should have been a simple job, nothing more than watching from a safe distance and noting if he left his address.

'She's gone.'

Helen stood up. 'Gone? What do you mean, gone?' Had the woman left her post? Helen was ready to flare in anger.

The voice at the end of the line shook. *'Dead. It's . . . it's such a mess.'* Helen sat back down suddenly, and her mouth fell open. *'So much blood.'*

'Ma'am, you need to assess this call.'

Helen rubbed her tired eyes. 'What call?' She didn't have the strength to stand.

'Aggravated burglary at a house on the edge of the same industrial estate where we found Robins. Occupants discovered a man with a gun in their house and he made off with their car. They said he looked *disturbed*.'

'I bet he fucking did. George Elms, you piece of *shit*!' Helen's voice was close to breaking. Everyone in the room had turned to her for some sort of direction. Hatred and rage brought back her strength. 'It's our man. Vehicle details?' she snapped.

'A 62 plate, white Audi S3.'

'Helicopter?'

'Main Control have contacted them. They are in the air, ETA less than five minutes.'

'Okay, good. Come on then, people, where's that piece of shit going now?'

CHAPTER 33

Whitfield had started life as a quiet village on the outskirts of the town of Dover, but the ever increasing demand for property in the area had seen it increase in size and importance so that it was now merging with the town. Whitfield also had an industrial estate, which contained a Tesco superstore, numerous garages, the district council offices, and a nondescript grey warehouse which had no markings.

At the warehouse, a security guard patrolled the sodden grounds in a high-visibility jacket, a cigarette burning between his lips, with his German Shepherd sniffing around at his side. A Vauxhall Vivaro van sat among numerous other cars in the customer parking area of the Vauxhall dealership next door. The tinted windows concealed a gang of five men, all pulling balaclavas over their faces and readying themselves for their task.

Ed Kavski's voice was muffled behind his balaclava. 'Okay, let's not fuck about.'

* * *

Harry was ex-police. The move to the security services suited him. He was quite happy to spend the night shifts napping or watching movies on a battered old portable DVD player. Vincent, the police dog that had retired with him, would lie next to his partner of seven years, some part of his body always touching his master. Harry had been a fantastic dog handler, something of a legend, and Vincent had been a large part of that. The German Shepherd already had the name Vincent when he came to him, and at first Harry hadn't liked it at all, but it had grown on him and had come to rather suit the dog. Right from the beginning, Harry and Vincent had clicked, and after their first meeting Harry was the only officer that Vincent would work for.

Harry finished his cigarette, coughed, and made his way back towards the rear door of the warehouse. He went inside and walked towards the office where his DVD player was on pause and the kettle was still warm. He passed a silent forklift truck, asleep among the rows and rows of floor-to-ceiling shelving stacked with pallets of unmarked cardboard boxes. The warehouse belonged to the ferry company, P&O, which ran out of Dover. It used the place to store several million pounds worth of cigarettes, perfumes and spirits. The company relied mainly on the building's anonymity to keep its stocks secure. And Barry and Vincent.

CHAPTER 34

White lines flashed under the Mercedes Sprinter van that had maxed out at 105 mph. Inside, the van buzzed with the voices of the division's tactical team, chattering as they prepped for the operation ahead. Only the driver was quiet. His eyes were narrowed, picking out road signs, looking for his exit, one ear on the radio updates that were coming in through all five radios turned to maximum volume. The front seat passenger was turned sideways so he could talk to the three officers standing in the back of the Sprinter, each of them desperate to get to the area, find the stolen Audi and stop it any way they could.

They had been warned not to engage if they located him. This was not an armed tactical team, yet the fact that their prey was armed and happy to shoot at police officers did nothing to dampen their enthusiasm.

The van was some way behind the team's sergeant, who was driving a marked Skoda Octavia VRS estate response vehicle. The police car had come to a stop with the engine ticking over.

'I'm just saying we need to think about it. Every other fucker's rushing to where the car was last seen, but it ain't gonna be there still, is it?' Constable Robert Miller, nicknamed *Windy*, rubbed his bald head, looked up from his map book and peered out into the dark night. Rainwater ran thick down the windscreen that showed the reflection of an intense Sergeant Ben Knotts.

'Well what options do we have? He's been seen taking that car so he isn't just going to take it home and pull up on the drive, now, is he? So maybe he's running as far from the scene as he can get. What else can he be doing?'

'He ain't running.' Windy was looking at his map again.

'What makes you so sure of that?' Knotts peered across at his colleague and friend.

'You said it, mate. He knows the police are after him, he's chosen a white Audi S3 — I mean even in rush-hour traffic, one of them would stand out. I don't think he's running at all. I think he's going somewhere, and he probably knows that there's gonna be coppers there.'

'What, some sort of final shootout? This ain't some fuckin' cowboy film!'

'Nah, mate. If he wanted a shootout he woulda just sat there and waited for us to come to him. He's running somewhere. It ain't home, so where else is there?'

'His wife, you think?' Knotts rubbed at his chin. 'All right, we'll go with your whim, but I'm sending the van to join in with the area search down where it was last seen. And let me tell you, if we miss out on the job of the century because you fancy yourself as something out of *Bad Boys,* I ain't gonna be happy!'

Windy pushed the map over towards his sergeant, pointing a thick finger at a B Road.

'His missus has moved to the mum's, right? From where the shooting happened he'll take this road to get away from the scene as quickly as possible but he'll get off the main road here.' He pointed to a junction halfway along the B road.

Knotts pointed at the map. 'This is where Freddie got done.' He was referring to the sergeant gunned down while still sitting on his police bike.

Windy nodded. 'It was there somewhere. He knows this area.'

Knotts pushed the map away and engaged first gear. 'Can you let the van know we're taking a small deviation but they need to continue to Hythe?'

Windy updated the van over a private channel used only by the team. The atmosphere was tense as Knotts accelerated towards the back roads of Hythe. Windy didn't like silence, so he punctured it with a tuneless song.

'Bad boys, bad boys watcha gonna do? Watcha gonna do when we come for you?'

Their laughter echoed around the car as they sped towards their destination.

* * *

The Audi stood out as it was driven hard through the sodden landscape of rural Hythe and it damned near clipped the marked police car as it passed in the opposite direction.

'Fuck! That was it.'

Windy needn't have said anything, Knotts was already hard on the brakes, he jerked the Skoda across the road, the front dug into the hedgerow and he snatched at reverse gear to complete the turn.

Knotts had received his advanced certificate when he was still relatively young. He had a natural feel for cars and could drive them to their limits. Now he hung onto every gear as he caught up with the red tail lights ahead. His teeth were clenched in concentration. 'We've fucking got him, Windy!'

Windy radioed in. 'Zulu Two Zero, permission.'

'Zulu Two Zero, go ahead.'

'Control we are behind the white Audi, we are at Barrow Hill, top end of Hythe.'

'Received, confirm SD62 KMS an Audi S3, colour white?'

'Yes, yes. We're not close enough to confirm the registration but it's our man and he is aware of us.'

'Received. Confirm you have illuminated blues and the vehicle is now making off?'

'We might as well,' said Windy to his sergeant, who responded by pressing a button marked '999' on the dashboard. The raindrops on the windscreen suddenly shimmered in bright blue. 'Yes, yes,' he said into the radio.

This time there was a slight pause before the reply. Knotts knew this was the point where an inspector at the control centre would be consulted and could call off the pursuit. He was past caring at this stage. There was no way he was going to lose that car.

'Zulu Two Zero, you are authorised for phase one pursuit. The inspector has asked that you be aware that you are not, I repeat not, to approach the vehicle or any persons therein should they decamp, nor are you to approach the vehicle should it come to a stop. You are to keep with the vehicle and provide commentary on its movements only. We are calling armed officers to your location.'

Windy and his sergeant exchanged hurried glances before Knotts' attention was drawn back to the road, which suddenly veered to the right. Thick trunks of old trees at either side marked the start of a patch of Forestry Commission land. Knotts brought the clutch down and dropped to second gear. He pulled the Skoda's front end round a sharp bend, and as it straightened out, the red lights of the Audi were suddenly bigger — they'd made up a lot of ground.

'Zulu Two Zero, you are required to acknowledge the last, over.'

'Received.'

Knotts thumped the steering wheel. 'We've fucking got him, mate. I tell you, he can't drive that thing for shit.'

* * *

George had misjudged a corner he knew well. It swept around to the right and his approach had been fine, but he'd pushed the car too hard coming out, and he headed towards a high bank and a line of large trees. The wheels had grazed the bank, the front wheel lifting up and dragging sticks and slippery leaves out of the undergrowth, spilling them onto the road. He hadn't suffered any damage, but getting the Audi back straight had lost him time. He now faced a long straight stretch up a steep hill, and the flashing blue police vehicle was almost upon him. The Audi powered up the hill. The patrol car fell away a little but George knew that he was three, maybe four miles from his wife and daughter. Much of that was along twisty, single-track country lanes. The buzz in his ears was so loud it felt as though it was penetrating his mind. His eyes blurred every time he passed a lit up road sign, the rain making everything flare like neon. He was fighting off a migraine that he knew from experience could blind him.

He still had no idea what he would do when he got to his family. All he knew was that he had to reach them.

CHAPTER 35

'Where the fuck are you?' Helen Webb said.

Barry Lance could hardly hear the chief superintendent's words. He hesitated a little before responding. He wasn't used to being spoken to in this manner and he had to remind himself that they were all under pressure. He was in a Range Rover travelling at 120 mph.

His voice was gruff with tension. 'Outskirts of Hythe. We're zero five from the last reported position.'

'You've been kept fully aware?' Helen Webb was whispering now.

Lance could just imagine her, ducked in some dark little corner away from the control room, glancing furtively round in case someone overheard.

'I think so,' Lance replied.

'You think so? Two more bodies, Barry. Two more dead on my watch and we had this piece of shit in custody. We had him and I want him here again. This time there will be no mistakes.'

Lance frowned. 'There was no mistake last time. We got him in clean.'

'The mistake was letting him go.'

'That's not really our part of the game, ma'am. I'll get him back in for you. What you do with him then is entirely your—'

'Not this time.'

Lance didn't quite understand. 'Not this time?'

'This time you don't bring him in. This time you deal with him at the scene, Barry. Do you understand what I am saying? We cannot give this man an inch. He will not hesitate and I do not expect you to either.'

Lance looked at the driver. 'I do understand the situation, ma'am — at least I think I do. We are en route, ma'am, with weapons ready. Can you clarify what is required of us when we get there?'

'Barry, this is not a police policy conversation. We both know how this plays out according to policy. We back off him, try to talk him down and it takes all night to get the man into custody, and all the while he has ample opportunity to take out more officers. In the circumstances I think you can justify the use of lethal force.'

Now Lance ducked away. He turned to the passenger door and pressed the mouthpiece hard into his cheek. 'You want me just to take him out.' He glanced at the driver, whose eyes were on the road ahead.

'As soon as you get the opportunity. He doesn't walk away from this one, not under arrest, not injured. Not breathing.'

'With respect, ma'am, we are an arrest team. We make those sorts of calls on the ground.'

'This is not a normal situation, Barry. This is the very reason I brought you and your team in — I needed a job done.'

'And I will need to justify my actions.'

'You will have my full support for your actions. George Elms dies tonight, do you understand?'

Lance shook his head. 'Understood.'

Helen Webb hung up the phone and turned to see Inspector Price approaching her.

'Ma'am, the helicopter's picked him up.'

Helen followed Price back to the control room and took up her position. Her throat felt dry and sore. 'Do we have video?'

Price nodded. 'Just waiting for it to buffer.' Helen bit her bottom lip as the live, birds-eye view of a speeding blur appeared, flashing through a canopy of trees. The picture was grainy, but it was good enough. The camera moved slightly and she saw the pursuing vehicle with its roof bar flashing blue. It was close, close enough to catch. And that might cause Helen problems.

'He'll be on Stone Street in less than a minute. He's heading for his wife.'

Helen spun towards the voice. 'Where is his wife?'

'At her mother's address, ma'am. She was moved earlier this evening.'

'Who authorised that?'

'We thought you had.' The stricken detective looked round the room helplessly. No one looked back.

Helen now focused on Inspector Price. 'So George Elms knows where his wife is, but the senior officer leading the investigation has no idea?'

Inspector Price shrugged. 'Maybe there's still people in the force that will talk to him. We've got an armed officer with her, he must have made the decision to move her. Your firearms team have just joined Stone Street off the M20. Elms is a few minutes in front of them, but he won't make it. He'll never get anywhere near his wife.'

Helen was still shaking her head when she made her transmission. 'Zulu Two Zero, Zulu Two Zero, this is Chief Superintendent Helen Webb. Are you receiving, over?'

There was a pause. '*Go ahead, ma'am,*' said Windy.

'Kilo Quebec are in position. Two Zero, you are required to break off your pursuit of the vehicle immediately. Confirm your understanding, please.'

* * *

'What did she say? Fuck! She's not cancelling us?' Knotts was watching the brake lights of the Audi as it came to a junction and turned left onto Stone Street. He knew the road well. It was long and straight and the more powerful Audi would have an advantage, but there were some twisty stretches towards the end, and Knotts was confident he could stay with him. There was no way he was going to let this fucker go. Helicopter or not, he wanted to be on hand for when Elms lost it and decamped. Knotts wanted to be there to put his hands round his neck.

'She said it, mate. We've gotta call it off. The chopper will take over.' Windy had leaned forward to try and get a view of the sky.

'I'm not letting it go. Not now. We found him.'

'Yeah, well done, but she don't give a shit about that, does she? We'll stay behind it — just ease back so we can pick up the pieces.'

Knotts had reached the junction. 'We stay with it.'

Windy looked at the radio handset in his hand, a little desperate, as it blared again.

'Did you receive the last? You are to cease the pursuit immediately.'

Windy pressed the button. 'All received.'

'What did you say that for?'

'Because *I* did receive her.'

Knotts said nothing, but he kept the Audi in his sights.

* * *

George screwed his eyes tightly shut for a second, just to see if the pain behind his eyes would ease a little, enough for him to be able to focus. Through the sodden windows the scenery was now flashing past at 110 mph. The rain had relented, but was now back hard and large droplets pierced the tree canopy. The night sky was split apart by lightning. The ringing in George's ears was so loud he couldn't hear the thunder. George knew this road well. He would have to turn off at the Six Mile garage, where the road surface would deteriorate considerably. After that, the road would lead him right round to where he needed to be, on the north side of Hastingleigh.

The Six Mile garage was shut for the night but still relatively well-lit. He could see that the patrol car had fallen behind on the straight, but he was sure they would have seen him turn in. Well, his cards were on the table as far as the police were concerned. He was going to see his wife and child.

Even if it killed him.

* * *

'Kilo Quebec One, Kilo Quebec One. Subject vehicle is left, left onto an unnamed road towards Maxted Street, the marked vehicle is close behind, also left, left.'

Helen Webb swore loudly. 'Zulu Two Zero, this is a lawful order. You are to break off the pursuit immediately. Do you receive?'

'Zulu Two Zero, received the last. We will break off the pursuit. Could you please confirm with Kilo Quebec that they will be continuing. We are heading towards a considerable electrical storm.'

The helicopter crew were quick to answer. *'Kilo Quebec One on the last, that's a yes, yes. We are aware of the conditions but the storm is still some distance away. There is no need to break off at this time.'*

* * *

Knotts was leaning forward, grimacing at the huge drops of rain now hitting the windscreen. The tree tops were suddenly etched against the sky in a whip of lightning.

'Some distance away my ass. We're fucking in among it, ol' son.'

Windy was also staring out of the window. 'I'd say so.'

'There's no way I'm breaking away from this.' Knotts sat back in the driver's seat and squinted at the brake lights ahead. They had got closer since the lanes had become tighter.

'Mate, she sounds pretty pissed off.'

Knotts cast a glance at his mate. Beads of moisture had formed on Windy's brow, and his body was rigid with tension.

'Look, I'm the sergeant and I'm the one operating the pedals. It's all down to me. I'll say you told me to stop. Don't worry.'

Windy narrowed his eyes, looking into the torrent, the wipers a blur. 'I am telling you to fucking stop!' But his tone was mild.

Knotts merely smiled.

* * *

George Elms could feel he was getting close. Visibility was getting worse as the rain became increasingly torrential and the windscreen wipers could no longer keep up. The Audi had slowed and George was aware that the car behind had made ground. The Audi's headlights picked out a very old and gnarled oak tree split down the middle, which he knew marked the start of Westfield Wood. George had spent many hours in these woods walking the in-laws' dog in the early days of his relationship with Sarah.

George drove to the tree and braked late and hard, but the pursuing vehicle made up more ground, so that just a few metres separated the two vehicles as they both exited the corner. The Audi scrabbled for front wheel traction on the sodden carpet of leaves beside the steep mud banks. The police Skoda lurched forward, making contact with the rear of George's vehicle. Both cars increased their speed but the Skoda came level with the back seats of the Audi. The road opened up. George knew that the police driver would need just another few feet on him and he would be able to make tactical contact, forcing him over to the side where they would either grind to a halt or spin him from the rear so he would lose control.

George's throbbing eyes flicked to his speedo. The needle rose quickly through 50 mph. He would have to take his chances on the straight. He knew he had less than 100 metres before the road became a single track and he would have to be clear of the Skoda.

The Skoda still urged forward in his mirror. It was just a few metres short but George's more powerful car was starting to pick up.

The cars accelerated into the darkness.

* * *

'What's going on?' The policeman had woken up the whole house. Sarah's mum had insisted on putting on the kettle, despite the initial message that they were being moved again, and as a matter of urgency. This had now been downgraded to a possibility. Sarah's mum swigged a steaming mug while Sarah stood at the open door with her arms folded. The house was surrounded by trees. The paved drive that led directly away from the front door led into a tight country lane and the only break in the treeline. Sarah's armed guard was staring in this direction.

'You look like you're expecting some awful monster to burst down that road any second now, guns blazing. It's ridiculous.'

The officer was poised. He looked ready for action. The butt of his rifle sat in his chest, and his finger rested near the trigger. The officer had been quite friendly all evening but he was ignoring Sarah now.

She tried again. 'Officer Toner. Billy.'

'Sorry, Sarah, I'm trying to stay in touch with the radio so I know what's going on. I've told you, you really need to be back in the house.' Billy tapped at his earpiece.

'You can't just say there's a threat coming to my door and expect me not to ask questions. We've already moved once tonight. How would George even know I'm not at home anymore?'

'As soon as I have any answers, I'll tell you. We're not moving for now. There are more officers coming over, you will be perfectly safe.'

Sarah sniffed. 'I could have told you that. This is ridiculous. If George is coming here, fine. Let him. I'll make him a cup of tea and find out what all this is about. 'Cause I can tell you now, he isn't the person you people seem to think he is.'

Sarah's mum tugged at her daughter's sleeve. 'Come on, love. Let's go back inside for now. Billy here will let us know the second something happens. We might as well make ourselves comfortable.'

Sarah huffed, but she allowed herself to be led back to the reception room at the front of the house, which they called the snug. It had a huge fireplace, and low-slung, soft leather sofas, one of which held a sleeping Charley Elms.

'Go and lie down with your daughter.'

'This is ridiculous. I should never have agreed to leave my home or to have an armed guard. Guarding us from what? I don't like guns.'

'The police know what they are doing. They may be being a little overcautious, but rather that than not doing enough. We just don't know what's going on with George at the moment.'

Sarah glared at her mother. 'Don't you start.' She sighed, wriggled onto the sofa and wrapped her arms around her daughter. Charley slept on.

* * *

They were doing 60 mph when they got to the trees. George knew the road and was ready. He swung into the middle, his nearside wing mirror scraping thick branches, where he made contact with the Skoda, forcing it into the dark woodland. Both cars braked hard, and both lost control. George's Audi surged ahead. He clipped the right bank and over-corrected, veering into a sideways skid. The Audi rode up the steep left bank and turned over. It bounced upside down back out into the road, where it collided with the opposite bank, spinning back out into the road again like a bowling ball in a buffered lane. Bits of the interior were smashed loose. George was thrown about, helpless.

The Skoda's demise was a lot more sudden. The front end struck a thick tree trunk. The front airbags exploded in the faces of the two police officers, but their legs and lower bodies had no protection. Knotts' legs buckled under the pedals and the steering column while Windy hit the dashboard hard. Branches punctured the windscreen, ripping at the two men and tearing through the car roof.

Both vehicles came to a complete stop in a sudden silence. They rested twenty metres apart. No one moved.

Three minutes behind them, Barry Lance and his tactical team turned off the main road and headed towards Westfield Wood.

* * *

'What was that update?' Helen's face was stern and tense. She had been standing most of the night and she was still upright, she clamped her headphones to her ears.

'*Crash, crash!*' The helicopter, Kilo Quebec, was back on the radio and continuing with their excited updates. *'Both vehicles have lost control, the lead vehicle is on its roof, the police car has entered the trees, no signs of movement at this time.'*

'Fuck!' shouted Helen. She pulled her headset off her head, ready to throw it to the floor. Then she took a deep breath and hooked it back on.

'*Foxtrot Six, we are zero three from the location. Confirm there is no movement from the subject and no visible threat at this time?*'

The helicopter crew replied immediately. '*There is no movement, both cars took a big hit, there will be casualties. Can we get an ambulance running?*'

Helen looked at an operator who was already on the phone trying to explain the exact location of the crash site. They exchanged nods.

'The ambulance is on its way, but until we have confirmation either way, we are still treating George Elms as an armed threat.'

Helen hoped Barry Lance took this as a reminder that he was expected to complete the job — if the car crash hadn't done it for him.

CHAPTER 36

George was not immediately aware that he was upside down until he felt for his belt release button and fell in a heap onto the roof. It took some time before he was able to shuffle into a sitting position. He had taken a significant blow to the head and it leaked blood. He touched the cut, feeling for signs of a fracture. It seemed okay. The door was crumpled inwards, and was jammed shut. He moved across to the passenger door, which had suffered less in the crash, but it still took some effort to push it open. As he slid backwards out of the door his left hand brushed against cold metal — the pistol he'd been given that had been sitting on the passenger seat. He grabbed it and thrust it into his pocket.

Swinging shut, the door caught his right foot, and what was already a painful ache became an excruciating flash of pain. George yelped. He pulled himself far enough away from the Audi to get a view across to where the blue lights of the patrol car still flashed. The front grill lights had gone, smashed to pieces against a large tree. There was no sign of life. Gingerly, George moved backwards to the steep bank. His head thumped and he could hear nothing but the ringing in his ears, which was louder than ever. His head hurt. The blood was thick on the side of his head. He managed to push himself up against the soaking bank until he could stand on one foot. His whole body ached.

George took the gun out of his pocket and attempted to assess his options despite the roaring in his ears. Whatever he did, the outcome looked bleak. The area would be crawling with police and they would know where he was. He could stand still and be arrested within the next few minutes, or he could walk the half mile or so to his wife and child. If he reached them, he would be searched and shackled but they might just let her see him for a few moments. In that brief time he could maybe get a message to Sarah, try and persuade her of the danger they were in. That they couldn't trust anyone.

It was his only option. George peered into the depths of the Westfield Wood. He would have to stick to the road, but could he even walk? He tried putting some weight on the damaged foot and cried out. His foot seemed to be at a slightly wrong angle. He tried to hop on his good foot, putting as little weight as possible on the other, but the pain was so intense it nearly knocked him over. He wanted to cry, to curl up in a ball where he was and just give in. But he would never have another chance. George managed to move, in a sort of hop and drag that was just about bearable. Progress was slow, but every step brought him closer to his family.

* * *

'Foxtrot six show us arriving.'

Barry Lance and his team of seven had reached the scene. It was surreal, unearthly — carnage lit with a blue strobe. Four officers made for the stricken Skoda. Two had their gun barrels pointed towards the upended Audi, while the others were carrying medical equipment. The remaining three were listening to the updates from above. The crew of the chopper could see clearly through their infrared camera that George was limping away, and the men felt they had a little time before they set off after him. Leaving the two medics to do their work, the five remaining men started to jog in formation towards Elms.

It didn't take long before the lurching figure was in their sights. Lance had the voice box. 'George Elms, armed police, stop where you are and put your hands out to the side!'

George was walking up the middle of the road. His right foot dragged behind him as he made his way towards the house. The rain persisted, the trees above offering some slight shelter for the men spread out across the road, each projecting a red dot onto George's back. The dots moved and danced as George limped on.

Lance lowered the voice box and radioed to the helicopter crew above. 'Foxtrot Six to Kilo Quebec, can you give us some light please.'

The helicopter activated a 'Nightsun', a 50,000 lumen searchlight that made the area around George into broad daylight. The armed officers could now clearly see the blood running down George's right side, soaking his white T-shirt. They saw the black, short-barrelled pistol in his right hand.

George squinted up at the source of the intense light then quickly looked down. He stumbled, trying to stay upright, his head movements seemed to have thrown him off. His right foot struck a large stone, which had been dislodged from the bank in the torrential downfall, and he clearly recoiled in pain. But George Elms kept going forward.

* * *

'Drop the weapon, drop the weapon now, George, or we will open fire!' Helen Webb had opened up the microphones of the officers at the scene. She was still standing up, and her fists were bunched, her head slightly bent as she listened intently. The video feed from the helicopter had frozen, occasionally jerking forward, but it was useless. She could hear all of Lance's team shouting at George to drop the weapon. Now was the time to take him out. If he did as he was commanded and dropped the weapon, there would be little justification for putting a bullet in him. She needed it done now.

'Fucking shoot him!' A couple of operators standing close to her turned and stared. Helen no longer cared. The world would be a better place without the murdering bastard. *Her* police force would be safe.

* * *

The red dots still danced on the back of George's shirt. No one wanted to shoot him in the back. George was holding a weapon, he had demonstrated his willingness to shoot and kill police officers, but he was no threat to them now.

'Take him out.' Helen Webb's voice came through the men's earpieces. This was against protocol. It was their decision, but Helen had authority. Their fingers tightened on the trigger. Still they hesitated.

'Take him out! What are you waiting for?'

The men slowed their pace.

'This man's a killer, he is armed. Take him out!'

Barry Lance knew he had to act. He broke from the formation and ran forward. 'Hold your fire!' he shouted. His men watched as their sergeant stopped five metres short of the subject, his weapon raised.

'Drop the weapon, George!'

* * *

George knew officers were behind him, certain to be armed, but he hadn't heard their instructions. He was no threat to them and he thought that if he just kept walking they might keep their distance, allowing him to get close enough to the house for his wife to come out to see what the commotion was about. It was a desperate hope. He became aware of someone coming up close behind him. Close enough he could make out the words they were shouting. George stopped.

'Drop the weapon. Drop the weapon and turn slowly!' Lance was three metres away, looking at him down his sights. George's head thumped. It was all up. He wouldn't be allowed to go any further. His family would have no idea he'd even tried, they wouldn't know the danger. His whole body was in pain and he had already gone further on his injured foot than he thought possible. It was the end of the line, time for it all to stop.

With a feeling almost of relief, George lifted his arms out to the side, his right hand higher than his left, and turned. His eyes were closed against the light, and the cool rain ran down his cheeks. In his exhausted confusion he had forgotten he was carrying a weapon. Though he didn't realise it, it was now levelled at the pursuing officers. George was now a direct threat.

Barry didn't hesitate. He pulled the trigger.

Two barbed pieces of metal hit George full in the chest. They implanted themselves six inches apart, and 50,000 volts of electricity passed between them for five seconds. George hit the floor and almost immediately felt the surge of electricity again, this time it lasted longer. George's pistol had fallen from his grasp. His head lolled to one side as the shock finally ceased and he saw Lance trap the weapon under his boot. Lance lowered himself down to where George lay on his back. He looked up. Lance was a silhouette against the Nightsun searchlight.

'You're under arrest. For cold-blooded fucking slaughter.' The sergeant's face was inches from George, and his spittle fell on his face as he spoke. 'Anything you say may be used in evidence. Have you got anything to say, you piece of shit?'

Lance's radio was still on open transmit as George managed to bring out his words.

'I did it. I killed them all.'

CHAPTER 37

Helen Webb walked out of the incident room. Her head was spinning and her body, suddenly relieved of the tension, sagged. She leaned forward and rested her head against the cold plastic of the coffee machine. She didn't want a coffee but she needed to get away and collect her thoughts.

Was tonight a good result? George Elms was off the street, and he would be for some time. He'd admitted to the crimes that had rocked the county over the last few days, but they'd lost so much, so many, getting to this point. They'd had him once. They should have let him rot in the cells but they'd been forced to let him go. Firearms should have taken him out this time, removed a poisonous cancer from her police force so she could start rebuilding. But they hadn't, and what now?

She knew there would be extensive investigations into what had happened tonight. Ultimately Firearms would be applauded. They had made the right decision. George Elms had been arrested with the minimum possible force — killing a suspect created a lot of paperwork.

Helen also knew that the tapes of the radio traffic would be part of the investigation. She could expect questions as to why she had ordered a firearms team to shoot a suspect. It was overzealous at the very least, conspiracy to murder at worst. It would depend on what angle they decided to take.

Helen sipped at the coffee. It tasted like shit. She reckoned she would be okay. She would be able to downplay her part in tonight's incidents. Emotions had been running high, there were many factors that would affect the judgement of even the most stoic of commanders. That's the line she would take. She would even play the female card a little — tears in the right places, the loss of Sam, a fellow WPC — she could use that. She'd probably just get moved to head up the training department or something similar, something out of the firing line for a little while. She'd seen it happen often enough.

'Ma'am?' The voice made her jump. 'There's been another job that's come in. They've asked that you be made aware.'

Helen turned to face a nervous and exhausted-looking operator.

'Another job? God, what is it now?' Her throat tightened. Surely no more loss of life?

'An armed robbery at P&O's storage depot near Dover. They've made off with a high-value haul and the security guard's hurt pretty bad.'

'A storage depot? This has nothing to do with George Elms, has it?'

'Well, no, ma'am. I was just asked to make you aware as the senior officer on duty. They even killed the guard dog.'

Helen Webb found a smile. 'Dead dogs and robberies. Well, by the cold light of day that will most definitely be someone else's problem.' Helen took another mouthful of foul-tasting coffee, and her gaze moved away into the darkness. She was suddenly aware that her messenger was still there, shuffling awkwardly from one foot to the other.

'You can fuck off now,' she said. And smiled broadly.

CHAPTER 38

Farthing Common. A beautiful spot at any time but maybe more so in the silence of the early hours of the morning. From this elevated position the North Downs slipped away, a vast valley bathed in the silvery light of a strong moon. Kane Forley waited in the carpark, his motorcycle tucked in among the trees. Behind him stretched a huge area of woodland that was popular with dog-walkers and nature enthusiasts. At night it was the perfect place for a private conversation.

'So this couldn't wait?' Billy Toner arrived just a few minutes after Kane. He was a rider too, his bike an American-style cruiser.

'I thought you would be happy. We all want to get paid.'

'This wasn't about the money for me. I wanted that piece of shit punished for what he did, just like you did.'

'Sure it wasn't. He did get caught, then?'

'He's in a prison cell. Or at least he will be once they've finished with him at the hospital. Admitted it was all him — just like you said he would. He's beaten up, by all accounts, but nothing lasting — shame. I hear he took another couple of us out tonight too.'

'Shit, really? Anyone you know?'

Billy shrugged. 'We'll hear all about it in the debrief I'm sure. Local patrols I think. I gotta be back in early doors, I reckon we've got a lot of writing to do.'

'You're ready to explain your actions, then?' You're going to need a cover story for moving the wife.'

'I panicked. There's been a lot of confusion and miscommunication tonight. I made a decision to move her on my own, worst-case scenario I get words of advice. I've not done anything wrong.'

'Fine then. You seem to have it all worked out.'

'That the money?' Billy gestured at a large rucksack resting against Kane's feet.

'Yeah,' Kane's smile was visible in the moonlight, 'but it's not about the money, right?' Kane tugged at a zip.

'It helps. Seriously though, I'm glad I could be part of helping you out, you know, after what he did to your brother. I didn't know Riley myself, but he was one of us and the lad was just doing his job.'

Kane had been looking down into the bag, his right hand inside it. He stopped and looked up at Billy.

'Riley . . . yeah. He was a good man. So, twenty-five thousand. I bet you've already spent the other half?'

'Not yet, I got plans for the money, but for now it needs to stay at the back of my wardrobe. That sort of cash can bring unwanted attention.'

'Yes, it can.' Kane took a firm hold of the pistol concealed in the rucksack. He angled it upwards, moving it as close to Billy as he could, before he could react. He fired one shot, it was almost point-bank. It struck Billy in the neck, his face contorted to confusion then panic as his breathing immediately became laboured. He fell to the floor clutching at his neck as blood oozed onto the ground.

'Sorry, buddy, you have to die by yourself. Another bullet from me and it wouldn't be suicide would it?' Kane said, standing over him.

Billy grabbed at his throat, his eyes wide, reflecting the moonlight.

'You just couldn't live with what you did, could you? Once you realised what you were part of. They'll find that money, Billy. They'll know what you did and why. But at least you did the right thing.'

Kane smiled. He squatted down by Billy as his movements finally stopped. His eyes staring at nothing. Kane pulled a cloth and a thin blue rubber glove from his pocket. He rolled the glove over his right hand and cleaned the gun with the cloth. He then used Billy's right hand to point the gun skyward and fired it again.

Kane stepped back to admire his handiwork. It certainly looked to him like a suicide. Whether it would stand up to a full investigation was another matter, but Kane very much doubted there would be one. Yet again he had given them an easy way out.

Kane slipped off the glove and lifted his phone to his ear.

'I'm expecting good news.' Ed Kavski sounded tense.

'What's good news for you?' Kane said, in the mood to play games.

'I'm busy, Kane, what's your update?'

'Elms is in hospital. He admitted killing those officers. Next stop prison.'

'He was supposed to fucking die tonight, Kane. We had an agreement.'

'What can I say? Your old lot must have bottled it. He'll take his prison time and with his mouth shut, because he knows if he doesn't, I will kill his family.'

'You'd better hope that's enough.'

'It's enough, I saw the fear in his eyes when he faced losing them. Besides, we all know you have your influence with Lennokshire Police. They needn't be looking anywhere else and you can make sure of that.'

'What about your inside man?'

'He won't talk. Nasty suicide. Poor chap.'

'So it's done. We also had an agreement that you would disappear too, Kane. I trust you will be keeping to that part at least.'

'Of course.' Kane chuckled, 'like all the great magicians.' Kane ended the call.

THE END

Thank you for reading this book. If you enjoyed it please leave feedback on Amazon, and if there is anything we missed or you have a question about then please get in touch. The author and publishing team appreciate your feedback and time reading this book.

Our email is office@joffebooks.com

www.joffebooks.com

LANGTHORNE SERIES

BODILY HARM

PANIC BUTTON

37027065R00132

Printed in Great Britain
by Amazon